"Almost there." Every step they took, Kate grew

"Where will we c

"At the main tra

Micah nodded. "Okay, that works. You have a car there?"

"Yes. Not much farther."

They moved into another area thick with trees that Micah recognized from years ago. Another couple hundred yards and they'd be to the trailhead. They just had to navigate this last section, steep with rocks littering the dirt pathway.

Kate slipped at the top of an incline, kicked one of the bigger rocks. Micah caught her, alarmed at the way he reacted to the feeling of her in his arms, even for a second.

He stayed still for a minute, with Kate, waiting for the rock to finish crashing down the hill, on edge and alert in case someone heard the sound and attacked them.

But the attack didn't come in the form he was ready for.

Instead a concussive blast shook the mountain beneath them, loosening more rock.

Kate screamed as the pieces fell together in Micah's mind.

Someone had set a trip wire for them.

Sarah Varland lives near the mountains in Alaska, where she loves writing, hiking, kayaking and spending time with her family. She's happily married to her college sweetheart, John, and is the mom of two active and adorable boys, Joshua and Timothy, as well as another baby in heaven. Sarah has been writing almost since she could hold a pencil and especially loves writing romantic suspense, where she gets to combine her love for happily-ever-afters, inspired by her own, with her love for suspense, inspired by her dad, who has spent a career in law enforcement. You can find Sarah online through her blog, espressoinalatteworld.blogspot.com.

Books by Sarah Varland

Love Inspired Suspense

Visit the Author Profile page at Harlequin.com.

ALASKAN AMBUSH

SARAH VARLAND

HARLEQUIN® LOVE INSPIRED® SUSPENSE

LOVE INSPIRED BOOKS

ISBN-13: 978-1-335-67898-0

Alaskan Ambush

Copyright © 2019 by Sarah Varland

All rights reserved. Except for use in any review, the reproduction or utilization of this work in whole or in part in any form by any electronic, mechanical or other means, now known or hereafter invented, including xerography, photocopying and recording, or in any information storage or retrieval system, is forbidden without the written permission of the editorial office, Love Inspired Books, 195 Broadway, New York, NY 10007 U.S.A.

This is a work of fiction. Names, characters, places and incidents are either the product of the author's imagination or are used fictitiously, and any resemblance to actual persons, living or dead, business establishments, events or locales is entirely coincidental.

This edition published by arrangement with Love Inspired Books.

® and TM are trademarks of Love Inspired Books, used under license. Trademarks indicated with ® are registered in the United States Patent and Trademark Office, the Canadian Intellectual Property Office and in other countries.

www.Harlequin.com

Printed in U.S.A.

Being confident of this very thing,
that he which hath begun a good work in you
will perform it until the day of Jesus Christ.
—Philippians 1:6

To my grandmother Kate Bryan. I borrowed your name
for this book heroine, and maybe a tiny bit of
your spunk, too. You've been in heaven for years, but
it didn't seem right to dedicate this one to anyone else.
Thanks for all you taught me.

Acknowledgments

To my family, THANK YOU for everything you do,
book related and not. I love you all. Thanks to my friends
for being supportive. Special thanks also to Mark and
Penny Agnew for that talk over brownies that helped
lead to this book. Mark, thanks for the information
about trackers—I tried to capture their spirit
with Kate's character, but any mistakes are mine.

ONE

The gunshot cracked loud in the snowy silence, confirming Kate Dawson's worst fear: someone wanted her dead.

So she ran. She didn't look around, didn't try to identify where it had come from, because it would almost be impossible to tell in the winter darkness with trees surrounding her, and if she didn't run, she might get hit.

Dying wasn't an option for her, especially on someone else's terms. No, if Kate died young, it would be from her taking her outdoor adventures one step too far, not from whatever it was she'd stumbled into when she'd gone home tonight. Whoever was after her had been in her house in town, had ransacked it completely, like they were looking for something. Kate didn't have what they wanted, didn't have a clue what it might be, but knew she needed to get out of there fast. Shivers had run up and down her spine on the walk from her house to her car; she'd known even then she was being watched.

She ran faster, legs burning as she powered through the powdery snow toward her cabin, the one place she might have a chance to escape. Kate dodged another birch tree and powered up the last hill before her cabin. Less than a quarter of a mile. She could do it, even with the backpack on her back. She'd never been so thankful to be in good shape.

As the bag slammed in rhythm against her back, she called herself every kind of fool for not mentioning to her brother Noah that she'd felt like she was being followed. She knew he was already worried enough that her home had been broken into. As chief of the Moose Haven police, he would have known what to do and would have mobilized the entire department to help her. Except she hadn't known what kind of trouble she was in, hadn't been sure if he could help and hadn't wanted to bring danger to her family's doorstep by going to their lodge.

So instead she'd driven around town, trying to lose whatever tail she had, and finally parked her car at the Hope Mountain Trailhead and headed for the safety of her cabin. Her plan had been to stay for a few days, try to figure out who could be after her and why, and alert Noah via the satphone she carried in her pack.

Something else to be thankful for in addition to her fitness level—she was always prepared in the backcountry.

Another pop and snow flew less than ten feet to the right of Kate. She could see her cabin now, not that it did her any good. Or did it? She might be able to hole up there. She had a .44 in her backpack in case any confused bears had awakened from hibernation for a snack. But that seemed like a bad plan. Unnecessarily dangerous.

Still, it was all she had. Get in the cabin, shut the door, get her own weapon out as fast as possible.

Fear clawed at her throat, made it hard to breathe, and Kate hated the sensation. She was rarely afraid for her safety—years taking risks in the backcountry had seen to that—but she hated feeling powerless.

She swallowed hard. Braced herself for the fight.

Because a person couldn't run forever—she'd spent the last decade denying that was true. But out here, facing a cold-blooded killer's bullets?

The only way through a problem was through it, just like her dad had always taught her.

With a last burst of speed, she made for the door, shut it behind her and took a deep breath before bending down to get into her backpack, remove the gun and the satphone. It was past time to call Noah.

As she did so, she looked around at her cabin, ready to assess the scene like she would in one of the disaster scenarios in one of the backcountry survival classes she'd attended for years. This was different than facing the elements, or even wildlife, but hopefully the skills transferred. They were all she had. The cabin was destroyed, just like the main floor of her house. The cushions had been ripped from the wood-framed futon that sat against the wall with the window that looked out into the woods. That would be the most likely place for an attack against her to originate from, if her assailant didn't come straight in the door. The drawer of the little side table had been pulled out and lay cracked on the floor and the books had all been pulled off her bookshelf.

Kate had her house, her car, her phone, a camera, this cabin. That was the extent of her worldly possessions, at least those that might be worth stealing. Not that this felt like simple stealing to her at all. This wasn't a crime of opportunity. She was being targeted.

Why?

She ran her hands along the cold wooden grips of the .44, took a deep breath and hoped she'd be strong enough to use it if she had to. Kate hated the idea of killing anything, especially a person, but if someone broke in here intent on killing her…she wasn't opposed to self-defense.

Another gunshot, this one so loud she knew her pursuers must be right outside the cabin. But if so, why hadn't it hit the cabin, shattered a window?

More gunshots, these farther away.

Kate tightened her grip on the .44, frowned. Two sets of shooters. Both shooting at her, or shooting at each other?

The shots paused.

The cabin door creaked.

Kate raised the .44, hands trembling more than she wanted to admit, and waited for her shot.

The cold of the snow was the first thing that registered in Micah Reed's mind when he came to. He blinked his eyes against the darkness, could make out the shapes of dark trees around him.

How long had he been unconscious? He rubbed his throbbing head, the blackness threatening to pull him under again. He wouldn't let it. He had to get up, get away from the scene of the ambush that had taken place. He and his partner had thought they'd been prepared to make this arrest, but something had gone wrong.

Micah focused on the pain in his upper arm, willing it to help him stay conscious, grounded in reality. It gave him something to grit his teeth against, another reason to fight. He struggled to sit up, to get his bearings and figure out how far he'd made it from Jared Delaney's cabin.

His partner of three years was lying dead somewhere behind him, on the cold Alaskan ground, shot dead by criminals they'd been attempting to apprehend and arrest.

He still didn't know what had gone wrong, though there would be plenty of time to analyze every aspect later on when he had to fill out the incident paperwork. But right now all Micah knew was that they'd been so sure they had had what they needed to arrest Jared and Christopher Delaney to take them down for their part in a ring of thefts from several places in Anchorage: museums, high-end gift shops, even hotel lobbies displaying Native Alaskan artwork that the group later sold. They'd been confident the two brothers were the heads of the operation, though not desperate enough to pose a huge danger.

Of course every arrest had danger in it. Everything he did as an Anchorage police officer did—traffic stops included. It was part of the job, a risk inherent in it, and one Micah had accepted. He'd known one day he might die doing what he thought was right, protecting people who were more and more resentful of that protection.

He hadn't counted on losing a fellow officer, though. He'd assumed his commitment to not let that happen would be enough, would somehow keep those around him safe.

He'd thought wrong.

Micah swallowed hard. Thinking was good, it was better than letting himself fade back into unconsciousness, but he needed to get up, get backing this, do what he could to arrest them on his own. Now that he knew they were willing to kill…making the arrest solo wasn't ideal, but he'd do what he had to do.

He pushed himself up, the cold of the snow stinging his bare hands as he did so. His gloves… where…? That's right, he had taken them off when they'd approached the cabin and shoved them in his pockets. He felt for them now but they were gone. Probably lost in the pursuit, when they'd realized their tip was a setup and the Delaneys were waiting… When Stephen had gotten shot and Micah had managed to drag him away from the scene only to watch his life ebb away under a spruce tree…

He owed it to Stephen to make sure justice was done here.

Although…

He forced his mind to focus, to go back to the ambush. The one where they should have been able to arrest the Delaneys, put an end to their crimes and tie the entire case up with a nice bow. But the Delaneys' cabin had been guarded by far more than two men. He wasn't sure how many. Four? Six? Only three well-prepared and well-armed men? He didn't know. Easy enough to explain, as the Delaneys had men working under them. But something rubbed him wrong about that, his mind wouldn't let that answer be sufficient.

It hadn't seemed like the Delaneys were the ones calling the shots. They weren't the ones yelling orders; there'd been someone else, a man, but his voice was too foggy in Micah's memory to do any good.

Which meant they'd missed something in their investigation. Missed *someone.*

Micah rubbed his hands on his pants, glanced down at the blood running down his arm. The wound had stopped bleeding when he was still but had picked up some now that he was using it again.

He needed to get moving. He could feel the edge of his mind growing fuzzy, maybe shock setting in, maybe the beginnings of hypothermia, he didn't know. They'd come prepared for the hike to Jared Delaney's cabin but at the last minute he'd left his backpack with some gear behind in the patrol car. Time had been of the essence and he'd thought it would be better not to be weighed down by too many safeguards.

Stephen had protested, as usual. They balanced

each other out, Stephen's safety-conscious streak and Micah's willingness to take chances. They'd both had on their vests, should have been well enough protected had the Delaneys and whoever was with them not had such a high-caliber weapon. Why the round had hit Stephen and not Micah, who'd been only eighteen inches away, he didn't know. The men had been aiming at both of them, Micah knew that, but guilt still ate at him. Why Stephen? Why not him?

But he couldn't begin to think it through right now. He owed it to his partner to finish what they'd started.

He couldn't think about this anymore. He had to do something. Find the Delaneys. No—foolish with only one officer. Better to focus his energies on getting off this mountain—ironically enough, called Hope Mountain—and into Moose Haven to see a doctor.

He'd thought he'd be able to come down here for a few hours, arrest the Delaneys and leave. When he and Stephen had discovered the Delaneys' connection to the little Kenai Peninsula town and found evidence that their cabin on the outskirts had been used for illegal activities related to their theft ring, they'd thought it was a straightforward mission. Find the cabin, arrest the two brothers. No trip into Moose Haven proper necessary.

Nothing had gone as planned. And Micah felt like he'd been sent straight back to square one.

Now instead of avoiding the town and the people in it, he was going to have to head straight into the heart of his past, back where he'd been born and spent the first sixteen years of his life before his parents had moved to Anchorage for work and taken him with them.

Micah kept aware as he walked, scanning the woods, which were darkening. He glanced at his watch. Three o'clock, almost sunset here in the middle of January, at least not long before it. The darkness would make it easier for him to hike down undetected, but he didn't relish the idea of finding his way in the deepening blackness. He had a flashlight—*that* hadn't fallen from his belt, thankfully—but he couldn't use it without risking detection. Micah wasn't sure if they were after him or not, but figured there was a good chance. They wouldn't want to leave anyone alive.

He didn't like feeling hunted.

Micah crept along as quietly as he could, feeling keenly the difference between apprehending suspects on the city streets he was accustomed to and this kind of backcountry work. The last time he'd spent substantial time hiking on a mountain like this had been in high school, on this mountain, before his life had changed course dramatically. Back when he was practically an honorary member of Moose Haven's Dawson family.

He wasn't far from the Dawson lodge now. If he got down this mountain—no, *when*, because failure wasn't an option—the first place he'd go was to find Noah and talk to his friend for the second time in fifteen years. He'd called Noah last week to give him a brief rundown on the Delaneys, since it seemed they were using Moose Haven as a base of operations even though most of their crimes were actually perpetrated in and around Anchorage. If Noah had been surprised to hear from him, he'd hid it, treated him the same as he had when the two were inseparable, chasing each other through these woods playing cops and robbers, honing their sense of justice as they played as kids.

Movement in front of him caught his attention, off to the left in the trees. He squinted in the gathering darkness. One of the Delaneys, but he couldn't tell which. Where was the other brother? It was too much to hope for that he'd been injured during their earlier skirmish, because Micah had been coherent enough to know that only he and his partner had been hit by the bullets that flew.

He hated it when it felt like the bad guys were winning.

Keeping quiet, he crept toward the shadowed figure, followed him at a distance. Was he tracking Micah, but poorly? Or had he given him up for dead and was doing something else now?

That's when he saw another figure, up ahead in the trail, just obscured enough by a stand of trees to be safe for now, but wouldn't be for much longer if he or she was who Delaney was tracking. It was a woman, petite, but in excellent shape given the pace she was keeping. It wasn't quite a run yet, but close, and she held herself tensely, like any second she'd sprint away.

Run. He tried to silently will her, eyes darting from her to Delaney, both of them too far away from Micah to do any good.

As he watched them, his foot caught on something. He glance down—tree root—and in the time it took him to look back up, a shot was fired.

Had Delaney fired it?

Micah assumed so, because the woman, whoever she was, was at a sprint now. One of the brothers must have fired the shot. Her pace in this snow was impressive; Micah looked at where Delaney had been.

Nothing.

He'd lost him in the dim midwinter light.

Biting back his frustration, he unholstered his own service weapon, which was thankfully still at his side, and moved forward. His arm throbbed and he realized he'd be shooting with mostly one hand, since his other arm was not able to grip as tightly as he was accustomed to.

He hurried through the woods, staying parallel to the trail, watching.

The sound of another gunshot gave him a chance to pinpoint Delaney's location. There. Not far from the cabin the woman was running into.

Micah couldn't let him reach that cabin.

He fired two rounds at Delaney when he had a clear shot, thankful that the last bit of daylight was enough. Any darker and he'd have had no choice but to put his weapon away. Micah had learned gun safety here in the woods, from Alaskans who took their weapons too seriously not to be safe with them.

Delaney fired back, reminding him of earlier, outside the Delaneys' cabin. Remnants of the firefight echoed in Micah's mind and he swallowed hard, his partner's yell so loud in his ear he could almost promise it was happening right now.

He couldn't get derailed by that, had to focus on right now.

Micah returned fire. *God, help me keep it together. Make him stop shooting, and let me check on that woman.* His prayers were disjointed but sincere. He shouldn't be alive right now; that bullet his partner had taken had been meant for him. And this had been primarily his case.

God must have some purpose in keeping him

alive. And that meant He wasn't finished with Micah yet.

Help me, God.

Seconds passed. Nothing. Only silence.

Micah swallowed hard, moved through the trees toward the cabin, around to the opposite side where Delaney had been shooting. Darkness was almost all encompassing now, providing him the cover to get to the door. Hopefully.

He pushed at the door, surprised it wasn't locked.

And found himself staring down the barrel of a .44 Magnum.

Held not by one of the Delaneys, but by a woman who looked uncannily like a girl he'd known fifteen years ago. She wore a winter hat that her dark hair spilled out of at the bottom, in silky brown waves he'd always wondered what it would be like to touch. Her eyes were mossy green. Focused right on him.

"Kate?" He barely breathed the word, heart squeezing in his chest.

TWO

Of all the things Kate might have expected would happen in quiet Moose Haven, getting shot at was not one of them. She'd once longed for a life in law enforcement, and if that had happened, maybe it would make more sense. But right up there with being shot at was seeing Micah Reed again. That is, if the uniformed man in front of her, decked out in Anchorage Police Department gear, was Micah. Could the guy with the well-over-six-foot frame and broad shoulders really be the same kid who'd hung out with her older brother and practically been the third Dawson brother in two years of high school?

And then he'd just left. Not even bothered to say goodbye to her. Apparently she'd never been more than Noah's pesky younger sister, despite thinking they might have been friends.

Okay, and despite the fact that her ridiculous fourteen-year-old heart had harbored a small crush and wondered if they might be something more. When they were older. If he had stayed.

"What are you doing here?" She lowered the revolver slightly even as she glanced at the window, wondering if the person shooting at her was still outside.

Or if he was right here in her cabin. She raised the gun slightly again, heart pounding in her chest. It was impossible that Micah could be the shooter, wasn't it? Time could change people; she knew that better than most. She couldn't assume she was safe just because she'd known him years ago.

"You mind putting that away?" Micah stepped inside, letting the door shut behind him.

His voice was even, not in the least flustered, but he was out of breath and now that she'd had a minute to study him she could see that he was bleeding from one arm. Not the one holding his weapon, but his right hand.

"Are you the one shooting at me?"

"No."

"Do you know who is?"

"Yes."

Kate lowered the gun. "All right, tell me."

Micah shook his head, holstered his own weapon. "There's no time. I don't know where he went but he saw you come in here and you can be sure if he intended to kill you earlier, he's not going to leave you alone until he's…" His voice trailed off and Kate raised her eyebrows as she studied the expression on his face. If she'd had any questions about whether or not he still saw her as a kid, his friend's little sister, they were answered in his eyes and his hesitation. He was still trying to protect her, still saw her as a child, or at the very least like someone fragile who needed special care.

"Killed me?" she finished.

He winced like she'd hit him. Instead of feeling reassured, knowing that he did care about her well-being, she was frustrated. She was tired of her brothers treading lightly around her, trying to protect her because she was the youngest Dawson. Because she'd been through events that had almost taken her from her family.

Those things had happened after Micah had left town. But small-town gossip was a strong force and news had probably found its way to Anchorage. Now he'd be overprotective like all the rest. As long as he didn't whisper, like some people did, that would be enough for her. She'd heard someone in the grocery store just last week. *That's the one, Kate Dawson. She never did seem the same after that avalanche…*

"So what's the plan?" she asked him, because he knew who they were dealing with. Generally she preferred to be the one making decisions. A lifetime of leading search-and-rescue work had gotten her used to it.

"Stay out of the Delaneys' way until I can get back to Moose Haven and call for backup and arrest them."

"Who are the Delaneys?" Kate knew everyone in Moose Haven, at least the year-round residents. The town grew in size substantially in the summer and she didn't claim to know all the tourists who had seasonal cabins around the area. But this was winter. Not exactly high tourist season.

"It's a long story. Seriously, we have to go. He's out there somewhere."

"He didn't hit us earlier, so he can't be that good a shot." Kate tried to keep her voice even, rolled her eyes for effect, even though her insides were shaking. For all the high-risk situations she'd been in, she'd never been shot at before. She didn't like it at all. Put this adventure down on the "do not repeat" list.

"They killed my partner."

She swallowed hard, no response seemed appropriate. Her flippant comment about him not being a good shot stung now, but she didn't know how to make it right.

"I need your help, Kate. I wouldn't ask if I had any choice, and I'd rather just whisk you away and keep you safe and be some kind of super-hero, but I can't."

"I'm not asking you to—"

"I know. But I'm asking you."

"What do you want?" Again, she struggled with her voice, to keep her fears, her feelings out of it.

"We need to get off this mountain without getting shot. We need to get to town so I can report everything that's happened."

"I have a satphone. We can call now."

"It's enabled with tracking, correct?" Micah asked.

Kate saw his point. She had the phone off now, but when it was turned on she had it set to give regular updates about her GPS location. It wouldn't take someone exceptionally good with technology to access that data. And while she didn't know if the people after her were tracking her, it wasn't worth the risk.

Micah continued, "When we were kids you knew these trails even better than Noah and I did. You notice things other people don't, Kate. At least you always used to. Since I found you out here, alone, in the dark, I assume you haven't changed."

The admiration in his voice didn't escape her notice and Kate felt her face warm with the praise. Should what he thought mean so much to her still? Whether or not she wanted to deny it, it did.

But he was wrong about one thing—she *had* changed. But not in that way. She was still the best tracker Moose Haven had, and she appreciated that Micah remembered, had confidence in her that wasn't swayed by her small size, her gender. She'd had to convince more than one new SAR volunteer that she was, indeed, in charge of their team and capable of it. Kate nodded. "I can get us off the mountain."

"I'd appreciate it. If there was any other way, if I could lock you up here and know you'd be safe and find my way down alone…"

"But you can't."

"I know. But just…know that I would." He ran a hand through his hair. "I hate that I'm dragging you into this."

"You aren't."

The way he narrowed his eyes made it clear to Kate she wasn't the only one who struggled with past familiarity with someone warring against a suspicious nature. Micah Reed, suspicious? She could see him as a cop. He'd always wanted to help people and it was a way to do that, a noble one. But he had been one of the most trusting people she'd known, back then.

Maybe they'd both changed.

Maybe not for the better.

"Seriously, Micah." His name rolled so easily off her tongue, and she wondered for half a second how it would feel to start a friendship again with this man, who'd been one of her closest childhood friends—she'd always found it easier to be friends with boys than other girls. "Someone is after me. I'm already dragged in."

"Who?"

Kate raised her eyebrows. "The guy who was shooting at me. So are you going to tell me who he is?"

"Later. I have questions too, but if we don't leave now…"

Micah moved toward the door and Kate followed, then hesitated. "Actually maybe it's better if we stay. You know?"

"Why?"

"He hasn't shot at us lately. We have shelter here. He could be waiting outside the door."

Micah shook his head. "No. We need to leave."

"Why?"

"Call it gut instinct."

"I don't believe in instinct—I believe in observations and making choices based on those."

Was that a snort she heard from him? "Kate, come with me. I really think—"

A sudden shot shattered the glass, which rained down on the cabin floor in a spray of shards. Kate felt the world slow as Micah reached out, took her in his arms and moved between her and where the shot had come from all in one smooth motion. "Run. I'll follow you. But pick the best, most isolated path down this mountain that you can."

Kate nodded, and went for the door.

"On my count," Micah said as another bullet came in the open window and pinged off the edge of one of her metal stools. "One… Two…"

"Three."

She shoved the door open, stepped into the blackness.

Before her eyes had even adjusted, she began to run, determined to use every ounce of energy she had if it meant they could outpace whoever was after them. The moon had been full only a few nights before and even now as it was waning, providing enough light for her to see through the darkened shadows the trees created against the bright white-blue of the moonlit snow. Kate dodged a long-hanging branch, wound through the spruce trees and did her best to bury them so deeply in the brush that no one would be able to find their trail, despite the fresh snow. Even if someone did find the trail, Kate already had a plan for that. She could circle the area where they camped tonight, create some false tracks. Anything that would throw off whoever was following them.

Because they weren't getting off the mountain tonight. And Kate knew enough from her basic first-aid classes to know that even if he'd rather press on and play hero, Micah would need to rest at least for a short time to give his body a chance to recuperate. The gunshot was only the beginning of what he'd been through, if Kate's guess was correct. She had a small first-aid kit in her backpack that she never went into the mountains without. When they could stop, she'd do what she could for him.

"Go faster! Don't wait on me—I can keep up."

Kate had already been pushing as hard as she could—but she found another gear somewhere, avoided a tree root that curved upward enough it stuck out of the snow and took a sharp left turn.

"Be careful!" She barely raised her voice above a whisper, not wanting to give away their location, but wanting to warn him as the trail she'd picked suddenly sloped downhill. Kate kept running. She paused for a second at a drop-off, only about five feet, then climbed down it before picking up her pace.

A glance back now and then confirmed Micah was staying with her. She didn't see the shooter anywhere.

Kate didn't know how long she ran, only knew that by the time she felt she had no choice but to slow down, her heart was beating out a crazy rhythm and her lungs were burning for air. She took a deep breath of it, reached into her backpack pocket for her water bottle and took a long swig.

"Why did you stop?"

"Because some of us didn't have to pass a police fitness test and I needed to breathe."

"You're the very definition of an Alaska girl." He surveyed her doubtfully. "You aren't going easy on me because of my arm?"

In the chaos, the urgency, she'd actually forgotten about his arm for a little while, besides the reminder to herself that they'd need to stop eventually. He honestly seemed to be concerned that she'd gone too easy on him, though, which was nice. She'd rather be overestimated than underestimated and she'd had plenty of the second in her life, first as a kid trying to keep up with her brothers and their friends, and even as an adult woman working search and rescue.

"No, I have to breathe." She took a few more breaths then looked behind them, listening but hearing nothing other than the sounds of scraping spruce branches in the wind. For the moment, there was a brief calm.

Rather than being reassured, though, Kate felt her chest tighten, then her whole body. Her muscles were all ready for fight or flight, and probably would be for some time.

"Tell me who you were after. What are these guys like?" she asked around panting breaths.

Micah frowned. "I said we could talk later."

She shook her head. "Tell me now. Knowing a

person I'm tracking, knowing what they're like, routes they're likely to take based on what I can gather of their personalities—it all helps. I've never tried to avoid being tracked, but I assume it's the same concept in reverse."

He nodded in understanding, shifted on his feet as he thought. "Thieves and smugglers. We thought they were the heads of the organization but now it seems they're just extremely talented but lower ranking. No known activities besides their illegal ones. No legitimate jobs."

"Not from Moose Haven, right?"

"One of them has a cabin here, but no."

"They're from Anchorage then?"

"Wasilla. But their crimes have mostly been committed in Anchorage, with a few in other locations. Fairbanks. Juneau."

"Sounds pretty far-reaching." She nodded, running through criminal profiles again in her mind, trying to get a handle on what they'd be like. "All right, ready?"

"If you are."

She paused. "Can I see about your arm first?"

He shook his head. "Later. I want more space between us and whoever is shooting."

Kate started running again, hoping the people pursuing them would lose the trail in the darkness. She was almost tempted to pray; she was so desperate to not be caught. The idea of how close she'd already been to several bullets—she didn't want to think about it. People knew she was tough; she'd certainly heard her siblings brag about that many times and while it always made her smile, it wasn't entirely true. She was tough in one context—the woods and the mountains and the backcountry. The backcountry could kill you, but it was logical, usually played by the rules. Even wildlife behavior could be predicted to a degree and Kate had had several run-ins with moose and bears that had ended well for everyone because she'd understood the rules too and played by them.

These men who were after them now?

They didn't play by the rules.

And that was exactly why she was terrified.

Following Kate, Micah ran through the darkness, through the trees that were thick on this lower half of the mountain. He supposed he should be thankful they weren't above the tree line, where there would be no way to avoid detection and nowhere to take shelter.

The way he figured it, they'd have to stop for at least an hour or so later. Neither had to sleep if they didn't feel like it, but they'd need to eat and rest a little before continuing on. And he needed to pack something around his arm, since over the time he ran it leaked a little more blood. It wasn't enough to cause problems, at least he didn't think so, but when they could stop, he'd take better care of it. The pain was a wave of intensity as he ran, but with enough focus he could ignore it, power through it. It was when they stopped that the constant throbbing made him grit his teeth.

His mind turned to his partner again and he felt anger seethe in his middle. The arrest should have gone smoothly. They had done their due diligence to assure that it would and it had still gone wrong and they'd missed something, gotten a huge part of the case wrong.

Who had the third man been? The other man with the Delaneys? He wore a mask over his face, so all Micah knew was that he was a male of average build—not much to go on especially in a state where men outnumbered women.

He felt his frustration grow, this time with himself. Even with his partner, Stephen too, though that made him feel worse—once people were dead weren't you supposed to think only good things about them? Either way, neither of them realized there was a high-ranking third person involved in this operation; while Micah knew if he was honest that it hadn't been his fault or Stephen's that they'd missed it, the criminals had just hidden it well, it still burned that they'd made a mistake, been outnumbered.

Lost one of the good guys.

Micah shook the ache, the events of the last few hours out of his mind. The loss of his partner stung, cut deep. But this wasn't the time for grieving. He owed it to Stephen to finish what they'd started. Right now that meant focusing on following the woman in front of him. He'd never have thought he'd run into Kate Dawson up here, and wished in a way it was anybody else. Besides Noah, his best friend growing up, Kate had been his favorite of the Dawson siblings. He'd admired her daring, her ability to keep up even though she was two years younger than he was and even more years behind her oldest brother. She wasn't like other girls he'd known then and she wasn't like any women he'd met since.

He hated that she was in danger now.

Although if he was honest, she was one of the best-equipped people to handle it. The Kate he'd known years ago didn't back down, didn't give up. She seemed even tougher now.

And now that he was down one partner and running for his life, Kate was exactly the kind of person he needed on his team. Already she'd saved him from finding his way down the mountain in the dark, and her determined attitude was infectious too. He could use some more of it right now.

"I've got to stop soon."

Kate slowed her pace, came back to where

he was, looked around as though Micah himself hadn't been keeping himself highly aware of their surroundings and looked at his arm. "Pain getting worse?"

"No but the bleeding keeps starting up again."

She wrinkled her nose.

"You don't do blood?"

"It's not my favorite, but I can handle it." She looked to the right, then behind them. "We are about half a mile from where I'd wanted to stop. Can you make it that far?"

"Yes." Especially when he was looking at a pair of dark hazel green eyes practically daring him, challenging him.

He hadn't been fair to her earlier, when he'd thought about her as a kid. She'd always done more than keep up, just like now. She was the one who set the pace.

The half mile to Kate's planned stopping place was slower going than the trail had been earlier, and more than once a spruce branch that Kate had pushed back without holding it slapped Micah.

"I'm sorry. I'm usually alone—I'm not used to thinking about someone behind me."

"You just go. I'm fine. I can handle it."

So she'd listened. The trees were thicker here, and he suspected Kate wanted to make sure their trail was as difficult to find and follow as possible since they'd soon be stopping to rest.

Micah was already making plans for that—one of them would be awake at all times. Unless the situation changed for the worst, he might even take a quick nap. He'd seen the way Kate handled that .44. She could more than handle protecting them for a short time; that was how confident she'd seemed with her weapon. And it was a good thing because he needed a nap, at least half an hour. He'd lost count now of how many hours he'd been awake but it had to be edging toward or past the twenty-four-hour mark.

Just as he was starting to question how well Kate measured distance, the woods cleared. Something ahead of them made a hill in the snow, but he couldn't quite tell what. He looked around the clearing, but didn't see anywhere that seemed like a good place to stop. It would be difficult to find where someone would start attempting to track them from, with all the tight trails through the trees Kate had taken, but they also needed shelter. He didn't see anything that fit the bill.

"Where were you planning…" Micah trailed off as he watched Kate walk over to the mound and a grin spread across his face. A cabin. She'd found them an old cabin, sunken down into the earth and now covered with snow. They'd be protected, sheltered because no one who wasn't looking for this would see it, and warm. A good thing since they couldn't risk starting a fire for fear of being detected.

He glanced back at their tracks, noting how fast the still-falling snow was covering them. Another hour or so and all evidence of them being here would be erased.

"How did you know about this?" He didn't even try to keep the admiration out of his voice and Kate could tell too—he knew from the way she smiled back at him, obviously proud of herself.

"I've hiked all over this mountain, on every marked trail I've found and some unmarked ones." She shrugged.

"Why?"

Another shrug. "I like it out here. Life makes more sense."

Interesting. He'd love to follow up on that later. The Dawsons lived a charmed life—cozy lodge, warm family. Even though their parents had died, the siblings' bond remained strong and it seemed they'd all worked through their grief and were living pretty happy lives. Not like Micah. His parents had given him everything he needed in the physical sense, but their preoccupation with their jobs had kept them from spending time with him. As an adult he saw them maybe once a year. They always sent a Christmas card, though.

No, not like the charmed life the Dawsons lived at all.

What about Kate's life could she not make sense of unless she was in the woods?

He followed Kate's tracks to the cabin and helped her dig out the snow in front of the door enough that they could open it without letting a pile of snow into the structure, but not so much that it would make an obvious entrance to the snow covered mound if trouble did happen to follow them here.

"We should be safe here." She nodded, looked around one more time, then climbed down into the cabin.

Micah followed, closing the door behind him and looking around. There was a stove in the corner. The cabin itself was decades old and in disrepair, but there was a box of blankets in the corner that looked like someone had put them there recently, at least in the last few years.

Kate didn't seem surprised by the box.

"Did you put that there?"

She nodded. "I don't know how many other people know this place is here, but I figured if anyone got into trouble they could use some supplies. Not everyone is as prepared as they should be out here."

"Is that something your parents taught you? I

don't remember them spending too much time in the woods."

Kate seemed to consider the question and finally nodded. "In some ways, yes. You know they loved it up here, but they didn't venture into the woods often, so they didn't teach us everything we would eventually need to know. I sort of just learned from experience."

Her tone said there was a lot behind the word *experience*, but she didn't owe him stories of her high school years and later. He'd been the one to leave town and no, he hadn't had a choice about that, but in an age of internet and social media, it wouldn't have been hard to keep in touch. He'd been the one to choose not to. He hadn't wanted to watch her grow up into the woman he'd already been able to tell she was becoming when he left. While they'd only been friends, his feelings toward her had started shifting just before he left in a way that made him resist the idea of watching her fall in love with someone, get married, raise babies.

And know that it wasn't him.

He swallowed hard, the truth about his past feelings for Kate something he hadn't wanted to deal with then, and still didn't want to deal with now. It was better if he kept her at a distance, though being back in her town and in such close proximity was making that a challenge.

Kate spoke up, saved him from his own mind. "Some of my experience has come through search-and-rescue work. That takes up most of my time." It was like she'd read his mind and decided to answer at least one of the questions he hadn't asked. Micah was grateful. She spoke up again. "Tell me a little more about who these men are and why they're after me."

"I wish I could do the second, but I have no idea. You've never met the Delaneys before? Either of the brothers?"

"Not that I know of."

"Tell me everything about today, what happened before you were shot at."

She met his eyes, seemed to be considering whether she was ready to talk.

Micah clenched his jaw. Did his best to wait. Someone was after her specifically, but he didn't know why the Delaneys could possibly have something against her. From the investigating he'd done, it was clear they didn't spend much time in Moose Haven, so they couldn't have interacted with Kate, at least not often.

So why target her?

He'd thought earlier that his day couldn't have gotten much worse, with the case in a tangled mess he didn't know if he could untwist and his partner dead. But he couldn't have imagined someone after Kate, a woman he cared about more than he should.

More than as his friend. More than as his other friend's little sister.

But the day had gotten worse. Knowing Kate was in danger made it hard to breathe, but it sharpened his focus, made him want to do a better job on this case.

He had to because her safety depended on it. And he wouldn't let her down.

THREE

Kate pulled a blanket tighter around herself and leaned against the cabin wall. She didn't remember the last time she'd pushed herself that hard physically and it felt good. No wonder her sister ran around mountain trails for fun. Today was almost enough to convince Kate to take it up herself.

If only she'd been doing it for fun, and not to save her own life. She shuddered, tried to push the past twenty-four hours out of her mind, but she knew she shouldn't bother. Micah needed to know what had happened, for the sake of his investigation, and she was the only one who could tell him.

Time to admit defeat and do it. Almost. "I'll tell you as soon as I call Noah."

She'd just reached her backpack when Micah stopped her, his hands coming down on hers. "Stop."

"I need to tell him where I am." She stared

at him, trying to figure out why he wouldn't let her… "Oh. Right."

"Your satphone will give the Delaneys something to trace."

In all her efforts to make sure they weren't tracked, she hadn't thought of electronic issues. Micah had mentioned it earlier but she'd forgotten.

Micah seemed to read the look on her face. "Is it on?"

Kate shook her head. She was thankful for that at least. She'd been in too big of a hurry when she packed her bag to power the phone on. Her siblings would have said God was taking care of her. Kate didn't know. "No, it's off."

"We should be okay, then, but don't use it."

"My siblings will worry."

"Better that they worry tonight and have you get back safely tomorrow than make them feel better now and tell the Delaneys our exact location."

She nodded and pulled the blanket tighter around herself. Her hands had started to shake slightly. She gripped the blanket and took a deep breath, willing her body to calm down. "Everything about today was normal until lunchtime."

"What happened then?"

"I'd been out this morning, at the lodge taking some pictures to include in the new brochure

Tyler and Emma made up to advertise the lodge. I went home to get lunch and my house had been torn apart. Drawers open, mess everywhere and furniture cushions slashed, just like at the cabin here."

It had been jarring, helping her brother and new sister-in-law, seeing their excitement over the shots she'd gotten, and then finding the destruction at her house.

"Someone trying to threaten you? Warn you away from something?" Micah asked.

She shrugged. "Could be, but it looked more like they were searching for something. Any idea what?"

She studied his face, but he gave nothing away with his expressions. Something he'd probably learned from being a cop, because when he was a kid Kate had been able to read practically every thought on his face. She'd never told him that, but apparently someone had pointed out his lack of poker face and he'd fixed it at some point in the last few years. It disappointed her, and then surprised her that it had.

"Did I tell you what the Delaneys are accused of doing?"

"Yes. You didn't mention any violent crimes, though. Do they have a history of assault? Or murder?"

"Not until today." This time she could read

his face. His partner. She winced, almost feeling his pain for herself, shutting out the memories that threatened to overtake her. They were always there, waiting in the edges of her mind, no matter how high she climbed, how many rivers she white-watered down, how many ocean passages she kayaked.

But she'd probably never give up trying to outrun them.

"They do kill people that get in their way, though." Kate said the words to ground them both, focus them both back on the present.

Micah nodded slowly.

"How did I get in the way?" She tried to wrap her mind around it, come up with some kind of working theory, but couldn't settle on anything. She'd had a low-key week, besides more rescues than usual due to the avalanche conditions. Four backcountry skiers had needed to be rescued within the span of five days and two had died from injuries suffered in the avalanches they'd been caught in.

Every single loss hurt. Kate took every one personally, despite the fact that she told the new SAR recruits to never do that. Mountains and avalanches weren't sentient, weren't out to get anyone.

But when it came down to it?

It sometimes seemed that was the truth.

Micah hadn't offered any new thoughts, yet, so Kate used the silence to go back over her week again, see what she could be missing. Had she acquired something they needed to search for? Had she talked to one of them unknowingly? The avalanche rescues did tend to attract crowds and one of the Delaneys could easily have been in one of them.

But that didn't give them any motive to kill her.

Unless… She wondered…"Do you know all of the people involved in whatever kind of criminal group this is?"

"We don't. We're missing quite a few people."

"I'm going to give you two names. Both of them area skiers I tried to rescue last week and both died. Different avalanches. Gabriel Hernandez and Jay Twindley."

"You think they might be connected?" He'd taken a seat beside her but he sat up a little straighter now. Kate nodded.

"I don't know how but…it's the only explanation for how I could have gotten on anyone's radar, at least that I can think of." She felt her eyes narrow. "Gabriel. Look him up first because we know how the avalanche that killed Jay Twindley broke loose but the one Gabriel was caught in was remotely triggered and something about it felt…off to me."

"That would be unusual, wouldn't it? For an avalanche to be used as a way to intentionally kill someone?" Micah asked. She appreciated that he was able to follow her train of thought without long explanations, because she wasn't good at those. Didn't enjoy them.

"Extremely." She shook her head. "I don't know if it's likely at all. But it's all I've got. I don't have anything of anyone's. I know that much." She looked over at Micah, met his eyes and found so much familiarity there, even after all these years, that she looked away. She hadn't let a friend get as close to her as Micah since Drew.

And Drew had died. She hadn't been able to save him.

Making friends had been harder since then.

She looked away from Micah's eyes, from the gut-wrenching, heart-cleansing kind of honesty she was tempted to proclaim when she looked there. She wanted to tell him everything that had happened since he'd left, how it made her feel, all the things her siblings had asked that she hadn't been able to articulate, things the counselor she'd seen exactly once had mentioned but she'd not been interested in discussing.

In her struggle to avoid Micah's eyes, his arm caught her eye. They'd both forgotten about it, though she didn't know how Micah had; it must be hurting intensely.

"Let me see what we can do for your arm, okay?"

Before he could answer she'd already pushed the blanket off herself and moved to a kneeling position. Her backpack had some basic first-aid supplies in it and she should be able to do a better job with it than what had been done so far— not a difficult proposition, since that added up to exactly nothing.

"Take your jacket off." He did so without complaint and she rolled her eyes. "You have on a short-sleeved T-shirt."

"I would think that would make what you're doing right now easier."

"Sure, yes, it does." Kate tried not to laugh but failed. "But I can't believe you're not hypothermic. You're from here—don't you remember how to dress in the woods in the winter?"

"I wasn't planning to be in the woods for this long."

"No one ever is. Be more prepared next time."

She felt his gaze without meeting it. She knew she'd sounded too serious, given away too much, betrayed the terror that *still* lurked inside at the idea of being unprepared.

"This is going to hurt a little." She cleaned the wound the best she could, thankful that while it was worse than a graze, it was just on the edge of his arm. She didn't have any experience doing first aid for gunshot-wound victims, but this seemed like it wasn't as bad as it could have been. She handled it the best she could, then looked over at Micah. Hopefully he wasn't planning to use this time to catch up, because she was exhausted, and while part of her wanted to know what he'd been up to for the last decade, she reminded herself that keeping him at arm's length was the best idea. He was here temporarily, just until he closed this case and then he'd be back to Anchorage. And the life she was living was in Moose Haven.

"We should get some sleep. At least one of us." Her shoulders sank with relief at his words. No small talk.

"Sure, go ahead."

"You can't sleep?"

Couldn't? Or wouldn't? In addition to the fact that someone shooting at her didn't do wonders for her ability to wind down, she didn't want to sleep in a room with Micah. The nightmares didn't come every night. They were down to just a few times a month. But she didn't want to risk tonight being the night she had one.

She shook her head. "Not yet anyway," she said to soften her words.

"Okay, you take first shift. Wake me if you hear anything off."

Her eyes widened. "You're seriously going to sleep?"

"I'm going to catch a nap, yeah. This cabin is secure, you have a gun and you know how to use it and I have no need to play hero and stay awake when it's not necessary. Wake me in an hour."

"Okay." Kate didn't argue, just sat there and watched him as he closed his eyes. His shoulders fully relaxed seven minutes later, not that she'd been staring at those broad shoulders.

Micah Reed was back in Moose Haven. Someone had shot at her.

Both improbable situations chased each other around her mind, like the irritating black miniature poodles her neighbors had. Eagle bait, she called them when no one was listening. If only the issues facing her now were as innocuous as those annoying dogs.

Neither made sense, unless one of the avalanches she'd worked recently had been caused by humans. In that case, though, why target her? She'd been the first one to the scene, but not the only one. Moose Haven Police Department had come too and as far as she knew, none of them were being threatened. She'd double-check with Noah to make sure, but that explanation didn't seem right to her at the moment.

Having thought through that subject, she moved back to Micah.

Yeah, she had nothing there either.

He was tall, handsome and all grown up, but still very much the same as he'd been from everything she'd seen in the last few hours. He didn't take himself too seriously, but he was sure of himself. Enough so that it didn't threaten his masculinity or his legitimacy as law enforcement to let Kate take the first shift while he napped.

She liked that kind of attitude in a man.

Or would, if she let herself spend any time thinking about men. About anything, really, besides work. Search and rescue had become her existence, the entirety of it. It was easy to justify. They needed her; it was her paying job; so many of the workers were volunteers... Blah, blah, blah. Her siblings usually addressed those issues when they tried to convince Kate to have a life outside it.

But that wasn't the reason she was a workaholic. Only Kate knew the truth—that saving lives was all she deserved to give her time to doing now. She owed it to Drew, for not being able to save his. And she had to stay focused.

The hour dragged on, and the quiet, usually something Kate appreciated, only magnified the thoughts in her mind that she'd rather not be wrestling with right now. When sixty minutes had finally passed, she set a hand on Micah's upper arm, feeling the firmness of his muscle beneath her hands. His eyes immediately opened.

"Your turn." He grinned at her.

Kate shook her head.

"Come on, close your eyes. Humor me."

"You're not the boss of me," she returned with a smile, but she closed her eyes, just to make him happy. And to make him stop talking…

Kate blinked her eyes open, jerked out of sleep and realized she'd nodded off. She stole a glance at Micah, who was looking around the cabin, seeming fully awake and watchful.

She trusted him to keep them safe, she realized as she blinked her eyes, more slowly this time, and let sleep claim her again.

Micah didn't know what surprised him more—the fact that he'd been able to catch a short nap while Kate was awake, or that she'd trusted him enough to nod off and sleep for almost two hours. She'd trusted him when they were kids, and there hadn't been this awkward distance between them, but years had passed. He hadn't earned her trust yet as an adult, something he felt the truth of deep into his heart.

She'd downplayed her own level of exhaustion on that run, or he just hadn't picked up on it, because she seemed drained in an extreme way.

"Ready to go?"

But she was in control again this morning, no hint of the shaking she'd experienced when she first realized she couldn't use her satphone and the reality of someone being after her had sunken in. Micah was pretty sure she'd be mortified if she realized he'd seen that; she appeared that committed to the strong, brave front she liked to put forward.

But she'd let it drop last night, just for a little while, even if it had been unintentional, maybe from exhaustion. There was something in her eyes that hadn't been there years ago, and it was more than just evidence that she'd grown up. She was different. It was as if she was more cautious inside. Eager to be prepared.

He glanced over at her, where she stood now without a trace of hesitation on her face.

She'd always been one of the strongest people he'd ever known but even she had a breaking point. He just hoped she was aware of that. Wondered if she was trusting God to help her or just powering through alone.

"I'm ready."

Taking one last look at the cabin that had been shelter when they needed it so badly, he sent up a quick prayer of thanks and then followed Kate back into the outside.

And almost ran into her. She'd stopped right outside the door.

"What—"

"Shh."

He stopped talking. Listened like she was doing but heard nothing.

"Let's go." She started walking and he followed.

The woods were easier to navigate in the daylight, but Micah was still thankful he had Kate with him because she took several turns down trails so narrow he'd never have seen them. Some of them were already packed down by animals, which would keep them from leaving tracks.

"How much longer to town?"

"We're close."

They walked for another hour in the woods before they came to a lower spot on the mountain that had more cleared areas. Micah felt his muscles tensing. It was the ideal location for an ambush. Would the Delaneys have realized they'd come this way? Or had Kate managed to lose them last night?

"I don't like how open this is."

She raised her eyebrows. "I don't like a lot of things about it, but if you want to get back to Moose Haven, this is the best way."

But she was tense too—he could see it in her jawline, in her shoulders. Still, he followed her down the slope, noting the way she kept looking all around them, head tilted slightly to the side like she was listening for something. Expecting something.

"You're worried about avalanches?" He was guessing but by the way she whirled around, he could tell he'd probably come close.

"I'm not worried about anything except whoever is after us. But there's nothing wrong with being cautious when conditions are ideal for there to be trouble."

So that was a yes, then.

With every step they took, she grew more circumspect and while Micah knew he hadn't been able to see well last night, he felt that the routes she was choosing today were a little safer. A little more careful than last night's sprint down the mountain at what could have been literal breakneck speed.

Thankfully they made it down without incident and Micah watched Kate relax a little more.

"Almost there."

"Where will we come out?"

"At the main trailhead."

Micah nodded. "Okay, that works. You have a car there?"

"Yes. Not much farther."

They moved into another area thick with trees that Micah recognized from years ago. Another couple hundred yards and they'd be to the trail-head. They just had to navigate this last section, steep with rocks littering the dirt pathway.

Kate slipped at the top of an incline, kicked one of the bigger rocks. Micah caught her, closed his arms around her out of instinct. They were closer than they'd ever been and his heartbeat quickened. Letting her go was the last thing he wanted to do, which was why he removed his arms the second she seemed to catch her balance. He never would have guessed he'd have reacted this way to the feeling of her in his arms, even for a second, even though he'd known his feelings had danced over the line between friendship and attraction. This was part of the reason he'd not returned to Moose Haven, even after he'd gradu-ated high school and had been free to. Because it didn't matter if he'd had a crush on Kate then or felt a slight attraction to her now. She was one of the Dawsons, a family who knew how to be there for each other, something he knew noth-ing about. Much as he'd envied their closeness when he was a kid, he knew he'd never be able to duplicate it if he ever had a family one day, and Kate deserved better. She was far out of his league, and he could only think of her like the little sister he'd never had.

They were only ever going to be just friends.

He stayed still for a minute, with Kate, waiting

for the rock to finish crashing down the hill, on edge and alert in case someone heard the sound and attacked them.

But the assault didn't come in the form he was ready for.

Instead a concussive blast shook the mountain beneath them, loosening more rock.

Kate screamed as the puzzle pieces came together in Micah's mind.

Someone had set a trip wire for them. Someone who could still be here, watching.

Waiting for them.

FOUR

Kate hit the ground hard after the blast, the snow softening the impact only slightly. Everything hurt, her head especially, since she'd fallen on it.

The darkness that had threatened to take her under was gone, though, and she managed to sit up, look around enough to see Micah beside her.

"What was that?" The question didn't encompass everything she wanted to know, didn't touch the depth of frustration, terror, anger that were clamoring inside her.

Because whatever the specific answer was, Kate knew all she really needed to. Whoever was after her wanted her dead. For sure, no questions.

"Trip wire."

So whoever had shot at her had been following them, but wasn't confident enough he'd make the shot to attempt another one? Kate could see that as a possibility. It was equally possible that whoever he was knew the area and knew this was the best way off the mountain.

She shouldn't have brought them somewhere so obvious. That mistake was all her.

Kate swallowed hard, pressed out against the heaviness settling around her at the knowledge that her decision could have gotten them both killed, not just her but Micah too. She darted a glance at him. She knew from their younger years that he'd view her as his responsibility. He and Noah were the kind of people who liked keeping everyone around them safe. They were protectors.

But Kate was too. And she couldn't live with herself if anyone else who was counting on her ended up dead.

She stood, started back the way they'd come.

"Kate."

She kept walking. He could follow or not, either way. But she wasn't going back to Moose Haven. Not when she didn't know who was after her, and didn't know if going back to town was going to put her family in danger.

"Kate." His voice was more insistent this time, but she wasn't a kid, wasn't his responsibility.

This time she whirled around, found him closer than she'd expected and stepped back. She hadn't heard him stand up and walk toward her, another bit of evidence that she was getting too emotional, letting fear crowd her brain. Situational awareness could be the difference between life and death and she was slipping.

She couldn't slip.

But she also couldn't go back.

"I'm not going to Moose Haven."

"Okay."

Not what she'd expected. High school Micah would have argued with her, tried to convince her to listen to reason, but this man version of him in front of her just nodded.

For reasons she couldn't explain, it just made her more frustrated. She turned around and kept hiking. She didn't lose her cool, not ever. More than once, one of her siblings had teased her about her frozen heart.

Micah Reed was not going to be the one to end her streak of keeping her emotions level and even-keeled no matter the circumstance.

As she hiked, she worked on her plan. They'd go back to the cabin where they'd stayed last night. She'd seen no evidence that its location had been compromised. Either someone had picked them up along the trail this morning and followed them enough to know where they'd try to come down the mountain, or they'd just correctly assumed that they'd take the best path to the bottom.

She was still frustrated with herself for that mistake. She'd debated this morning if she should tack some time onto their hike by taking a longer route, but after so long without bullets flying, the immediacy of the danger had dissipated some in her mind and she'd thought they'd be okay.

Obviously not.

"Where are we going?" Micah asked after a solid half an hour of hiking. She had to give him credit for how long he'd followed her without saying a word. It was more than she could say some of her siblings would have done. Noah would have followed her in the first place. Summer would have too, but then probed in her quiet way to figure out *why* they were going somewhere. Tyler would have tried to reason with her.

Micah just…let her be angry.

Wind whispered through the spruce trees they were hiking through as they headed back up the mountain. She'd have to turn soon, avoid getting above the tree line, where shelter would be difficult to discover. It was hard enough to find a place to feel safe here, the winter trees missing their leaves and the branches thin and skeletal.

No, this wasn't going to work. They needed to get back down, pick a new trail themselves if they had to, through the tangles of trees. This wasn't safe. She could feel it.

Kate stopped.

"Whoa." Micah ran into her, and she lost her balance. His hands went around her upper arms immediately, stronger than she'd realized they would be—not that she'd been thinking about such things—as he steadied her. "Are you okay?"

She turned to face him. He didn't flinch from her eye contact.

"No, I'm not."

The sound of a bullet exploded in the quiet.

"Get down!" Micah yelled, even as he tackled her. She hadn't been ready for it; the force of her body hitting the ground, so soon after the explosion earlier, jarred her, added a few new bruises she'd guess.

Kate kept her breathing even, reminded herself that she had to stay calm, tell her body not to react to the situation, but she would make decisions and act when necessary. It was not only part of her Search-and-Rescue Training, but she'd learned it when she'd been scouring books and online articles about law enforcement aptitude tests, years ago when her life had centered around another dream.

"Where is he?" she whispered, throat tightening slightly in spite of her effort.

"Can't tell."

Another shot. Kate listened like she was tracking something in the backcountry, then nodded to the right with her head. "That way."

"Is there anywhere we can go that has better shelter?"

"The cabin we were at earlier?"

"Closer."

"There's nothing closer but acres of wilderness."

Another bullet came close enough to them that Kate actually heard it whizz past, and a wave of dizzy nausea washed over her until she shook it off.

"No, there's…" She trailed off. The fallen tree, halfway between here and the cabin. It had left a hole in the ground where the root system had pulled out when it had fallen in a bad windstorm several winters before. "Maybe. It's halfway to the cabin, is that too far?"

"It's better than sitting here. Run as fast as you can, okay? I'll be behind you. Whatever you do, don't stop."

"Okay, unless you get hit and then—"

"I said, don't stop. No matter what."

Kate looked over at him, eyes catching his as some weird energy passed between them. Her breath stalled in her throat again. This wasn't one of her brothers, wasn't someone who should be willing to take the danger in the back. He was a friend, yes, but someone she had lost touch with years ago. She'd been another person back then, with so much less life experience. Much more naive. Hopefully.

He didn't even know her now. Didn't know

that she wasn't much, certainly wasn't worth dying for.

She nodded anyway, his expression making it clear that he wasn't taking no for an answer. "Okay. When?"

"Wait."

When another shot came, it seemed that was what he'd been waiting for because he whispered "now" and Kate ran like she never had before, not even last night. Last night she'd still been too stunned by the sudden danger to feel everything; now this heaviness was pressing on her chest, reminding her that this was real life, and just like the people who went into the snowy mountain unprepared and never came back, she was risking the only life she had.

The one she had could be over any second.

And she wasn't finished living yet.

A flicker of hope lit her heart as she ran. She was alive still. The regrets she had, it wasn't too late to fix them, was it?

She kept running, snow and leaves where the snowpack was thin crunching under her feet as she pushed herself faster, lengthening her stride as she jumped over exposed roots.

She slipped in one place, but Micah was there again, behind her to catch her almost before she knew she'd fallen. Rather than stop to thank him she kept going. She hadn't heard a shot in a few minutes but that didn't mean the shooter had given up.

No, she'd learned her lesson about assuming danger was past. Until whoever this was was caught, she was just going to have to watch her back. And Micah's.

Because she wasn't going to watch another person die. Couldn't let it happen again.

"Here!" Kate barely whispered the word as she dove underneath a fallen tree, but the intensity of her voice had his complete attention, just as much as a yell would have.

He'd never seen someone who wasn't law enforcement react under pressure this way. She wasn't superhuman or anything, but she was keeping her emotions under control. She was thinking, making decisions, while her life was in danger.

At the moment, he couldn't remember the last time he'd been so impressed with someone. Or the last time he'd been so thankful. He'd decided last night that Kate Dawson wasn't spending more than a few necessary minutes here and there out of his sight until the Delaneys were in custody. Micah didn't know how she fit into what they were doing, why they were after her or any of that, but he was sure about one thing. Actually two.

They wanted her dead. And that wasn't going to happen, not as long as he was alive to make sure of it.

God, please. I know You're the one who sustains life, but don't let me lose her.

Micah swallowed hard. There were more feelings in that prayer than he wanted to admit, a touch more than a desire to protect some random person would elicit. Of course it made sense. His friend's sister. An old friend.

"Come on." She reached out and grabbed his hand. Micah swallowed hard.

He'd yet to have an old friend grab his hand and cause this kind of reaction.

And he didn't particularly like it. Not when he had a case to work on, not when he knew that nothing would change who either of them was, the fact that even in a perfect world where no one was in danger, he would be the last person Kate Dawson should be interested in. He didn't have anything to offer her that would make up for having to haul her away from her family for the sake of his job, couldn't give her the life of stability she was used to.

Yeah, it was better if he ignored all his out-of-line reactions to her physical proximity. They were old friends. That was all.

His back scraped the bottom of the log as he climbed underneath.

"This is your hiding spot?" They weren't too concealed at the moment, but it was better than what they'd had. He nestled back against the snow and dirt, knowing they'd freeze if they had to sleep here overnight. This place wasn't sheltered enough, and even if Kate was hiding some kind of emergency shelter in that backpack, which wouldn't surprise him at all, using that would blow their cover and give away their location.

"There's a hole at the end where the root ball came out of the ground. We can easily make a shelter there with branches and should be able to make it look natural enough that no one notices it."

He raised his eyebrows. A shelter from branches. That was what they had as their plan to stay safe and wait out the people chasing them?

She could apparently read his thoughts because her face displayed every ounce of annoyance she seemed to feel toward him. "It's the best we've got up here. Unless you've got a cabin you aren't telling me about."

There was an idea. Hike up the mountain to where the Delaneys' cabin was, shelter there, wait until they came and then defend themselves if necessary.

Except Micah needed the Delaneys alive, if at all possible. First off, because they deserved to go to jail, pay for the crimes they'd committed, especially killing his partner. Second, because he needed to know they'd gotten the entire group of people operating the Native-art-theft ring. The pieces that had been stolen had cultural significance to several tribes in Alaska who had loaned the artwork to businesses and museums around Anchorage, but also, several museum workers had died under suspicious circumstances over the last eight months he'd been working this case.

Now that his partner was dead, now that Micah knew for sure that the Delaneys wouldn't hesitate to take a life, he owed it to those victims to look at their cases again, see exactly how they'd died and if the Delaneys had been responsible.

"This will have to do for now," he finally answered her.

"What's the plan after this? Your plan, I mean."

"Meaning you have your own?" He wasn't surprised by that. She'd never been the sort to go along with other people's ideas without thinking through other options first.

Something else he'd always liked about her.

"I asked you first." She didn't smile. And really, he couldn't blame her. He stopped smiling too, the gravity of everything that had happened settling down on him once again. The gunshots. The explosion. The face of his partner he hadn't been able to save.

"I need to keep you alive and get the Delaneys taken into custody."

"Those are goals—that's not the same as having a plan."

Note to self, she was feistier when she was scared. He hadn't connected the dots until just now, but that's what this even-more-abrasive-than-usual version of Kate was. She was afraid and since she hated that, she changed it to anger and irritation instead.

Interesting.

"We need to get to Moose Haven. I need to talk to APD, see if anything new has turned up in the investigation and pursue some leads I have after the ambush my partner and I experienced. I need to send someone for his body." Saying it aloud made him imagine his partner covered in snow, a punch to the gut. The man deserved better. But Micah couldn't change the past now. Couldn't let himself get buried in it.

"Before you can arrest them, right?"

Micah shrugged. "Preferably. I have enough to arrest them. They've committed a lot of crimes I know we have substantial evidence against them for, and getting convictions shouldn't be a problem. But I need to know if they're the ones calling the shots or if there's another member of this group we are missing so far. So I'd rather not arrest them until I have answers to that."

"That's fair." She paused for a few seconds. "So how are you going to get to that point? What's our best option for getting to Moose Haven alive and when we get there, will you go to the police department?"

"I'm still working on getting us down the mountain alive. You've helped with that so far."

She snorted. "I almost got us both killed taking the easy way down at the very base." She shook her head. "I should have known to take the threat more seriously. But they had stopped shooting…"

"And you stopped worrying?"

Kate shrugged. "Basically. I thought maybe we were out of the woods, so to speak."

"I don't know how they figured out where we were, but I don't think there's any reason to blame yourself. Honestly, I don't know that I could have gotten down without you last night. I needed you. We'll get back to Moose Haven, and you can stay at the lodge where people are around until we get this solved. I know how much you love being surrounded by people." He smiled a little, hoping to lighten the mood even just slightly with his snarky comment.

Kate's face didn't flinch. Not even a hint of a smile.

"What about my family, Micah?"

Oh. That was why.

The Dawsons were closer than any family Micah had ever known, though his experience as the only child of two professional adults who cared more about their jobs than their home life was different than hers by leaps and bounds.

It was one of the reasons he'd never allowed himself to entertain any serious thoughts he'd had about the embers of a crush he'd had on Kate since she was seven and he was nine and she'd shoved him down a hill after he'd made fun of the fort she'd built at the top of it. She had an amazing family, deserved to have one of her own one day.

And Micah had no idea how to even be part of a family like that. Especially now that he had a job that had him running into danger at unpredictable times. He thought of Stephen's fiancée. How someone was going to have to tell her that he wasn't coming home, ever.

Micah couldn't do that to a woman. Had never found one that would even tempt him to, and even if he did one day, what kind of love would that be, that would risk hurting someone else so deeply?

"Your family…" He dragged his mind out of the what-ifs, out of places it had no business wandering when they were who they were and he'd never be able to change that, and focused on the problems currently facing them.

Problems that honestly were big enough to

eclipse any other thoughts without much effort at all. Because the idea of Kate being hurt was unacceptable.

"I can't go to the lodge. But you could stay at my house, if you want."

He raised his eyebrows.

"Seriously? Come on. I'm not going within half a mile of my family if I can help it until this is over and I can guarantee they'll be safe. It's not a very big house, but there's an apartment connected to it, above the garage, that I've been planning to rent out to help out with income and it isn't rented yet. So there'd be a door and everything between us."

He was pretty sure she rolled her eyes at the last statement, which surprised him. She'd been raised with an even more solid faith foundation than he had, her perfect family filing into Moose Haven Community Church every Sunday that he could remember, minus the one where the siblings had all had chicken pox—probably thanks to Micah, who had spent an afternoon with Noah and Kate when he hadn't known yet that he had them.

"The door would make it look better."

"I'm not concerned about how things look—though I assumed you might be—I'm concerned with keeping my family safe and preferably staying alive myself."

"Those are the most important things." He nodded his agreement, hating the undercurrent of tension he could suddenly almost feel between the two of them, while at the same time being grateful that they at least had something to talk about instead of the awkward silence that had stretched between them for so much of the hike earlier. Micah wanted to ask her about her family going to church, though. See if things had changed for her, but something in her expression stopped him.

"What?" he asked as she studied him. She shook her head. "Seriously."

"Sometimes I can't read you at all anymore, and I can tell that you grew up and got law enforcement training and could probably make a career out of poker," she said. "But sometimes I can tell everything you're thinking. You're curious, aren't you? About why I could care less what people at church think?"

"Maybe."

Another eye roll. "You're not rocking the poker face right now, just so you know. I don't go to church anymore. Haven't in years. I don't see the point when I'm not sure if I believe anymore."

It didn't mesh, this new version of Kate and everything he'd known to be true about her. She'd been tenacious in her faith.

And he'd needed the strength God offered

him more in his adult life than he had as a kid. Couldn't imagine how someone could voluntarily live life without God's help. Was Kate trying to do that now? How could she have changed so much?

It wasn't just her faith in God faltering that rocked him, but the idea that she was grown up now—so far from the innocent high schooler he'd left, the one he'd pictured in his thoughts in the years that had passed when he'd allowed his mind to think about her, wondered how she was doing.

Micah swallowed hard, trying to shake the thoughts from his mind. He shouldn't care, shouldn't be affected at all by her choices. They were friends. That was all. Detachment—he needed to find it, now.

And then her hand was on his arm, not exactly helping his efforts to shut down his emotions.

"I haven't… I still… I didn't give up on all the principles and morals I was taught, Micah. So you can stop the assuming and fix that expression on your face." Her cheeks darkened a little and she looked away, then back at him. "I just don't know at the moment how I feel about a loving God who sits back and watches people die."

"Kate—"

"Shh. Did you hear that?"

She tilted her head up, to the side. Stared off

at the sky like she was tuning in to the wilderness itself.

She'd heard something.

Micah waited, hand on his weapon, heartbeat quickening. They hadn't come up with a plan yet for getting off the mountain safely. And it looked like they were out of time.

FIVE

Seconds passed, turned into minutes. Kate didn't hear anything else that indicated any other person was near them.

"False alarm." She whispered it anyway, not willing to take chances. She took a deep breath in and exhaled slowly, making an effort to release the tension in her shoulders.

"We need a plan. Now." Micah's tone was more sober than earlier and his expression matched. His eyes were a stormy brown, almost darker than the shade they usually were, if that was even possible.

Kate looked away. She might have harbored a ridiculous crush on him as a teenager, but they were adults now. Practical. And she had no business noticing his eyes.

She cleared her throat as quietly as she could. Nodded. "I agree."

"We can't stay up here."

"Right."

"But we can't endanger your family."

"Also right." She was glad he understood that. Her family's safety was nonnegotiable.

"So we need to get down from the mountain, get to your house in town and we can go from there. What's the best way to do that?"

"My family will be okay?"

"I promise—I will do everything in my power to make sure they stay out of it. Except…"

"You need Noah." It wasn't a question, but he nodded anyway. Kate knew he'd want his friend's help, not just because Noah was the police chief of Moose Haven, but because Micah trusted him. In a case like this where things kept getting flipped around, where Micah would come close to answers and then be left with more questions, he would need someone he knew he could count on.

Kate sighed as she nodded. "I understand. That makes sense."

"And of course you."

"Yeah, can't really keep me out of it at this point."

"No, I mean, you're part of the plan when we get to Moose Haven."

She raised her eyebrows. "How exactly is that?"

"I can't leave you alone."

"I'm a big girl. I can take care of myself." Although she was tired of having to fight so hard out here to keep a step ahead of the bad guys. Visions of camping out in her bathtub with a bunch of pillows and her .44, which she kept loaded for bear, danced through her mind, but that probably wasn't a practical solution to her safety issue. Eventually she'd need to sleep, more than the nap she'd caught at the cabin. She wasn't cocky enough to think that she would be able to function and think clearly without that.

So one way or another, she needed a solution. Micah might be able to provide that… But she hated to let him think he'd won.

"Let's not bother arguing about it," he said then, and she shot back immediately with her response.

"Because you can admit I'm right?"

"Because I've made my decision and I'm not changing my mind." He shifted a little, toward her, and Kate could see his facial expression even better. The set of his jaw, the steely tint of his eyes confirmed that as of right now, there would be no changing his mind. She had no doubts about that. She was about to speak up, argue again just because what else could she do, when he spoke first.

"We've got about four hours until the light starts fading again. Can you get us down in the dark if we wait here until then?"

Memories of the explosion from earlier rocked her mind again, a flashback of sorts.

She wouldn't be able to see a trip wire in the dark. Would he try that again? Was it a risk they could afford to take?

Then again, could they afford not to?

She thought. Stared at the tree trunk in front of her, the barrier providing them cover from being detected. And then nodded.

"Okay. I can do it."

"So what should we talk about while we wait?" he whispered with a small smile and Kate found herself wondering if he meant it, wishing that maybe he did. But she knew better. He was teasing her, thinking of her as a kid, like he always had.

And right now her emotions were already raw, on edge from the turmoil they'd been through the last couple days. She couldn't handle any more of it.

"I think we should be quiet. Less chance of being seen or discovered."

Just like that, the grin disappeared from his face and Kate could almost taste her own regret.

He didn't say anything else and she was left alone with the silence. And her thoughts. The biggest of which was that she wished she could go back, change what she'd said so she didn't shut him down, didn't leave him feeling like she didn't want to talk to him. The second biggest was that she shouldn't do that because it was playing with fire. He'd left years ago, been pretty clear about how he viewed her, which was just as a friend. She didn't have the time to be in a relationship anyway, with the rescue work she did. And she certainly didn't have any more of herself to give—the work took everything out of her.

Once again, as she had many times in the last few weeks, she wondered if the price was worth it to her.

And even if it was, how long she was willing to keep paying it.

Micah couldn't remember ever being so thankful for how fast dusk fell in Alaska's winter months. The darkness, like it had last night, would provide them a measure of cover, although it would make it more difficult to navigate the already dangerous rugged terrain coming down the mountain.

Right now, that risk was worth it.

They'd passed the last few hours mostly in silence. He'd been thinking through the case, making mental to-do lists and prioritizing what he'd need to do when he got back to Moose Haven. There was still no clear link in his thoughts between Kate and the Delaneys, but given how they'd destroyed both her house and inside of her cabin, he was planning to follow up on the idea that they were after something she had. It made as much sense as anything and gave him a lead to tug at.

A few glances Kate's way had given no hint about what she was thinking. Usually her eyes were closed, but he was pretty comfortable with his assumption that she wasn't sleeping.

She'd opened her eyes not long ago, looked around and muttered, "Thirty minutes and we can leave." And then closed her eyes again.

He'd raised his eyebrows at the time, at her confidence that she could pinpoint exactly when darkness would fall when he hadn't noticed her check a watch or anything. But she'd been right. Thirty minutes exactly. It was like she lived and breathed the outdoors, like the passing of time out here in the Alaskan wilderness was something she tuned in to as easily as most people could read words on a page.

"Ready to go?" he asked.

"Yes."

They stood, and he motioned for Kate to go first. She led them through the woods confidently, moving quietly. He kept brushing against branches, despite his best efforts, but he wasn't sure Kate made any noise as she walked.

She was like some kind of backcountry ninja. And while he could see how her savvy was useful in search-and-rescue work, he couldn't help but think of how useful she'd be in a law enforcement capacity.

He pushed the thought out of his head. Encouraging her to move to his line of work when he'd just lost his partner and been reminded firsthand of the inherent dangers of the job? He couldn't live with himself if he did that. He was trying to keep her safe. Not help her get through this so she could get hurt—or worse—another way.

Minutes passed, and hours. He kept alert for threats and could tell Kate was too, but nothing happened. Everything was quiet. Calm.

If only he could believe it would stay that way. He glanced up ahead at Kate, barely able to make out her profile in the moonlight as she made a turn on the trail and he followed. He had to keep her safe. Had to arrest the Delaneys without anyone else getting hurt.

And just like that, the idea of going any further tonight seemed like an abysmally bad one to him. They were both running on too little sleep, and even Kate's skills of observation were bound to be dulling by now.

"Stop," he whispered, and she did, turning around, eyes wide.

"What?" Kate whispered back.

"We need to stop for the night."

He watched her face as she considered him,

could almost see the arguments lining up in her mind, for and against listening to his opinion.

After almost a full minute, she nodded. "Okay." She looked around, nodded with her head to a cluster of spruce trees, tightly packed together. "In there?"

Worked for him. They could do what they'd done last night, each take turns sleeping while the other kept watch.

They moved quietly, without talking.

"You can sleep first," Micah told her when they'd huddled down amongst the trees the best they could. He was thankful they were packed tight enough that the snow around them, at least in here, was to a minimum.

She didn't debate this time, just nodded, pulled her winter hat down over her eyes and slept.

The night was quiet on Micah's watch. Not a sign of trouble. He even caught a glimpse of the northern lights overhead, between the spruce branches. He'd missed this. His apartment in Anchorage was too surrounded by the city lights to have seen them even if he'd remembered to look.

Soon his turn to rest came. Kate sat up, seeming awake and alert enough that Micah took his chance at sleep.

Morning came quickly, at least according to his watch. It was still dark enough that they could stay hidden, and he was glad for his decision to stop last night. They'd needed it.

"Ready to get off this mountain?" he asked Kate.

"Let's go."

They hiked for another little while, the trees growing even thicker as they descended closer to town. Soon they were going to have to get a plan together for how they were going to get into Moose Haven. Micah didn't relish the idea of walking along the roads into town with no shelter.

Kate stopped in front of him, turned round and whispered, "In five minutes I'm going to make a call."

"On the satphone?" There wasn't likely to be cell phone service where they were, though they were getting close enough to town that it could be possible. But the satphone was a better option. Whether or not the men after them would put the effort into tracking the call was a question, but with at least one murder under their belts, probably more if you counted those deaths Micah wanted to look into and the avalanche victims Kate had mentioned, Micah didn't want to take any chances.

His face must have answered for him.

"We need Noah to pick us up. The road back to town from where the trail we're taking comes out is too long and exposed. If they are waiting there, we won't make it. They'll pick us off without effort, almost."

He didn't like that option either.

He shifted his weight onto his other foot. "How many minutes before he'll be able to pick us up after you make the call?"

"We should all be able to meet up in less than ten minutes. Hopefully five, depending on how fast we go and where in town Noah is."

Micah glanced at his watch. After four o'clock. "Okay, do it."

"Not yet. We need to get a little farther." She started walking again, her pace even faster than it had been before, but Micah kept up easily, since his stride was so much longer. Still, last he'd known, Moose Haven didn't have a gym like the ones he and so many other officers used to keep in shape. He couldn't imagine how many hours Kate must log outdoors to be so fit.

"Okay." Kate stopped, slid the backpack from her shoulders and pulled the phone out. Micah felt his muscles tense as she did so, like somehow the very action of pulling the phone out would alert the Delaneys and whoever else they were working with to their location.

He didn't see anything out of place.

But that didn't mean they were safe.

"Noah, it's Kate. I'll answer your questions later but I need you to pick me up at the end of the gravel road near Hope Mountain… The one where we pick salmonberries in the summer, yes… Okay. Thanks… Be careful… Yes, now. 'Bye."

She powered the phone off and put it back in the pack, then slung it up onto her shoulders again. "Hopefully that won't come back to bite us. Five minutes and we should be okay." She started walking again, then turned back. "For now anyway."

At least he didn't have to worry about her underestimating the danger anymore. It was a small thing to be thankful for in the midst of a tangle of regrets, mostly that he hadn't been able to solve this weeks ago, arrest the Delaneys in Anchorage before they started going after Kate in Moose Haven.

They didn't talk much as they wove through the brush. Snow had started falling and was coming down thicker now, in large dense flakes.

"Good thing we're not higher up on the mountain. Avalanche danger will rise with snow like this." She bent and scooped some off the ground, as though she was testing the consistency, and then nodded like her theory had been confirmed. "Heavy and wet. Hopefully people will stay out of the mountains this weekend."

"Even if they don't, you won't be doing any search-and-rescue missions."

She turned back, raised her eyebrows, but said nothing.

"You are aware that you still aren't in charge of me, right? I'm not your pesky little sister you have to protect."

A sister? She thought he saw her like a sister? Everything in him wanted to correct that assumption, but it was probably better for both of them that he leave it as it was. Untrue as it might be.

"I want to keep you safe, Kate."

"Not your job either."

"Just don't make this difficult, okay?"

She snorted. Probably the best answer she could have given because Micah knew she had every intention of doing what she deemed best with no thoughts as to how much it stressed him out.

Even as he thought it, he felt the need to defend her to himself. She wasn't selfish; she just truly didn't understand that as much as she wanted to save the world through her search-and-rescue missions, other people wanted to keep her safe, out of the kind of danger she walked into on a regular basis. In a way, he was glad he hadn't stayed in touch because while he'd wondered about her over the years, he'd never worried too much. Kate was an adult and could take care of herself. But he hadn't realized just how many dicey situations she was putting herself into.

Micah heard a car's engine in the distance. They were at the edge of the road now. Close enough he knew how to get out of the low brush, but not so close that they were out of cover. He tensed, held up his arm to keep Kate behind him, ignoring the entire conversation they'd just had. "Stay back."

"It's Noah."

"Let's wait until we can see that for sure." She could make that annoyed face all she wanted, like he was overprotective, but as long as he was the one with the badge and the training, he was the one who needed to be making decisions about how to handle this investigation, and how to keep them both safe. Because like it or not, it *was* part of his job.

And the sooner Kate realized that, the better. He was already having to fight against criminals, one of whom had managed to keep his identity secret through a months-long investigation. He couldn't fight against her too.

Because if he had to, he was afraid they'd both lose.

SIX

They climbed into the back of Noah's police cruiser, and the first thing Noah did wasn't to greet Micah, explain who the unknown woman in his passenger seat was, discuss the case, which no doubt had made it across his desk by now, but to turn to his sister, even while the car accelerated down the road. Micah could almost feel his frustration.

"What were you thinking?"

Kate didn't appear the least bit intimidated by his tone. "I'm not your kid, Noah, so just stop, okay?"

"You can't just disappear like that. You don't tell someone that your house is ransacked and then just disappear."

"I did what I thought was best."

"You did—" Frustration was only building in Noah's tone. Micah knew he cared about his sister, knew that if he'd had a sister or any sibling at all, he'd understand that level of crazy protectiveness.

But he also knew from Kate's too-calm expression that she was about to be pushed a step too far.

"Hey, Noah, nice to see you too. It's been what, a decade or so?" Micah interrupted.

"Yeah, we'll get to that in a minute, you camping out with my sister in the woods while her family was terrified for her."

"Noah." The woman in the passenger seat shot him a look. "You drive. I'll find out what you need to know, okay?"

She didn't touch his arm, no physical contact at all, so Micah didn't think this was a wife or girlfriend. But she was comfortable enough to boss him around. Another police officer? Although wasn't Noah the chief? That would be pretty gutsy to tell her boss what to do, even in a situation like this.

The woman turned back. "I'm glad you're okay, Kate. We do need to know what happened, though." She turned to Micah. "And you are?"

"Officer Micah Reed, Anchorage Police Department."

She nodded, like she'd been expecting him to be an officer. "Trooper Erynn Cooper. I was with Noah when he got your call and figured you might be in the kind of trouble that warranted talking to the troopers."

Alaska State Troopers, huh? Explained why

she didn't hesitate to talk to Noah like an equal. Didn't explain the chemistry between them, but it really wasn't any of his business. And he had enough to worry about keeping his own personal life separate from work, at least as of the last couple of days.

Noah turned the truck to the left.

Micah saw Kate stiffen, watched her start shaking her head and start to argue. "No. I'm not going to the lodge. Turn around now or I'm getting out."

"Be reasonable, Kate."

"I am, Noah." For the first time, he heard her emotions in her voice. Anger. Fear. "I am being reasonable. I've been shot at, had a trip wire blow up down the trail from me, been shot at some more and I don't know why. I'm not bringing that kind of danger anywhere near my family. The only reason I called you at all is that we needed to get off the mountain so Micah could finish this case so it would all just stop, okay?"

No one said anything for a solid minute as Noah turned the car around in a direction Micah recognized as the road to town.

"We can go to the police department."

"That's fine if I need to make a statement or file a report. Then I'd like to go to my house."

Though he knew what Kate was thinking—that even though the criminals knew where her home was, they likely could find her anywhere in town and she'd rather be in danger herself than put her family in it. Micah still didn't love that idea and she could tell Noah didn't either.

"You can't stay there alone until this is over."

Micah spoke up again. "I'm staying in the apartment above her garage."

Noah glanced at Kate in the rearview mirror again, then turned his gaze to Micah. Micah met it without flinching. This wasn't just a childhood friend he was looking at. The man in the driver's seat was Kate's older brother, the police chief. He had every reason to be on edge right now and Micah needed his assistance, not just help keeping Kate safe, though there was that. He needed Noah's local resources to help him figure out who the extra man he was after was. And why he and the Delaneys were targeting Kate.

"She can't stay alone, Noah." He said it softly, hoping the knowledge that he was being protective too wouldn't upset Kate any more than she already was, but needing Noah to know that he was genuinely watching out for her and not trying to make some kind of stupid move on her. For more than one reason, that was the last thing he was planning to do.

"We'll talk about this later," Noah said in a low voice.

Kate bristled. "Anything you need to say you

can say in front of me, but let's not do it right now. Right now I want to know what you think, Noah."

"About?"

"My house. You went by there, right?"

"Of course. You said someone had ransacked it."

"Good." She nodded. "I hated to get you involved, but I did want you to check out the scene, figure out who had been in my house."

Again, Micah was impressed by her gut instinct, by the fact that she'd been calm enough to convey the information she needed to even when she was on edge. She hadn't handled it exactly the way he would have, with his training, but she'd done better than the average private citizen would have in the situation.

He guessed Noah approved too, because he went quiet for a minute.

"I did process the scene at your house."

His voice was quiet. Something prickled on the back of Micah's neck and he sat up straighter. Noah was talking to Kate, though. It was her house. So he stayed quiet, waited.

"What did you find?"

Noah shook his head. "Not what. Who. Well, sort of."

Micah shouldn't have, knew it, but he reached for Kate's hand anyway. She let him take it, made the slightest expression of surprise but tightened her grip as they waited for Noah's answer.

"We found blood all over your house. Someone was murdered there, Kate."

"Murdered?"

Even with everything she'd been through in the last twenty-four-plus hours, the news stunned her, sent ripples of fear and nausea through her midsection. She spent too much time saving lives for the town to lose someone to intentional evil.

"Who?" Kate needed to know.

"Don Walters," Noah answered.

"Why?" Kate hadn't meant to say it out loud, hadn't meant to think it even, but it was the question that echoed in her soul every time she lost someone in a search, each time she read another article in the paper about someone who had died young.

Every time she tried to fall asleep and saw Drew's face when she closed her eyes.

Why? Why? Why?

"We don't have anything else conclusive yet. Still waiting for the lab in Anchorage to get back to us on some of the forensics."

Kate nodded. She glanced at Micah. "Do you remember him? He runs...*ran* Don's Mountain Store. Had a bunch of outdoors stuff and espresso."

"I do remember."

"You found his body in my house?" She looked back up at Noah. He wouldn't have had any reason she could think of to be at her house, especially not inside.

"Enough of his blood on your floor to know his body is somewhere. The official word is that he's 'missing' but I saw the blood. Lots of it. He's dead, Kate. But you know the area around Moose Haven as well as we do. We may never find a body."

"How do you know it's him?" Desperation swelled in her throat as she thought of how kind he'd always been to her when she'd been in the store. Poor Don. Had he seen the criminals at her house and come to help her? Or come to warn her?

"His car was there, for one thing. The crime lab guys came down and took DNA also. That should be the conclusive evidence we need."

Kate turned back to Noah. Swallowed against the hollowness in her throat. "Will you let me know when you find out something?"

Noah looked in the rearview mirror, but didn't meet her eyes. Instead he was looking at Micah. He shook his head almost imperceptibly and she felt her shoulders tense.

"I may not be able to, Kate. You're not law enforcement."

"Is that the real issue, or is it whatever you and

Micah are saying to each other in your silent, secret code here?"

She turned to Micah to glare at him. Childhood friend or not, she didn't appreciate the way he was butting into her life, trying to make choices for her, thinking about how to keep her safe. She'd like to stay alive, yes, but preferably on her own terms. *She* was the rescuer. *She* was the one who knew the backcountry, was used to snatching people out of it barely alive.

She should be able to handle this herself.

"Noah. I'm asking you to keep me in the loop."

Her brother said nothing, was starting to seem like not her best choice for backup, so she looked over at Micah, who was studying her. Assessing her? He seemed to be measuring her somehow, but whether it was to see if she could handle being a part of the investigation, or something else, she couldn't tell.

She sat with her chin tilted up, eyes confident and met his without wavering. If he had any doubts that she could handle this, she wanted to set those to rest now. Kate knew she could. Nothing could be much worse than what she'd dealt with in the last day or so, except her family being in danger, but she wasn't going to let that happen anyway. She wouldn't let Noah involve any of them.

So yes, a tiny part of her understood why Noah

didn't want her to get involved either. And she appreciated his concern for her. But she was an adult, had been taking care of herself for a long time.

Kate didn't break eye contact with Micah, because he hadn't looked away yet and she certainly wasn't going to be the first one to do so. She needed to avoid even the slightest sign of weakness if she was going to convince them to let her be part of this.

Micah looked away. Never did answer her, and neither did Noah.

Kate looked out the window, watched as the familiar spruce trees slashed by as they drove.

The town came into view, a place where she'd always felt comfortable, and today she was shifting in her seat almost without thinking. How was it possible that it all still looked the same, from the snow-covered streets to the meticulously cleared sidewalks that the town was so proud of, to the buildings lined up in rows in typical downtown fashion...? Everything about it was the Moose Haven she'd been born and raised in.

But everything had changed. It wasn't safe here for her.

She looked away, looked in front of them at where they were going, focused on the Moose Haven Police Department as it came into view. After she gave her official statement, she intended to go home, whether Noah was okay with that or not.

Then again…would the police department have…cleaned?

Kate could handle a lot, but visible reminders of death always made it too easy for her to go back into the past, see Drew's snow-covered hair that he'd never run his hand through again. His blue lips, pale face. Chest that no longer rose and fell.

"I meant what I said." Micah's voice was a welcome distraction from her thoughts. "In the woods."

She felt her face tense into a frown, unsure what he meant.

They pulled into the police station parking lot.

"I'm not leaving you alone, Kate. Not until we figure out what I'm missing and I'm ready to arrest them all and get them out of here."

For some reason, this time she didn't have what it took to argue. Instead she smiled at him.

He looked every bit as surprised as she felt.

Kate smiling at him, on purpose, because she appreciated him watching out for her, was hands down the most unexpected part of the day, and so far, Micah's favorite.

Not because he had any kind of crazy romantic ideas. He knew better than that. But they'd been friends once, and a smile from her meant they had half a chance of becoming friends again, instead of her fighting him every step of the way while he tried to keep her safe.

They pulled into the parking lot of the station, and headed inside. Noah went first, then Kate with Erynn walking beside her, Erynn mostly making casual conversation with Kate—though Micah suspected she did so in order to stay close to Kate in case they needed to act quickly to keep her safe—then he was last.

He didn't notice anything out of the ordinary when he scanned the area. It looked like Moose Haven always had, but he knew better now. Somehow as a kid he'd assumed crime never touched their little coastal town, two and a half hours by car from Anchorage, tucked in among the bay and the mountains.

If he had anything to do with it, it wouldn't touch it for long.

More than anything right now, except Kate staying safe, Micah needed to talk to Noah, get a sense of whether his friend knew anything that could help him.

Micah took a deep breath. First this, getting Kate's report filed, making sure she was safe, and then he'd focus on getting back into the case. Playing offense instead of all this defense.

He watched her reach for the door, Erynn beside her.

A shot exploded. The door glass shattered.

Kate screamed and dropped.

"Get inside!" Micah yelled as he whirled around, put his back to Kate, trusting for now that Noah and Erynn would get her inside, but as the last man out, someone had to watch, find out where the shots were coming from. He had his weapon out but doubted he'd get a clear shot. It had sounded like a rifle to him, and the likelihood that the people after Kate had guessed her next move correctly, been ready for her, made him angrier than he could ever remember feeling.

Another shot. He caught a glimpse, a flicker, toward Bear Mountain, one of the large peaks behind the town. The guy had to be close to one thousand yards away. Micah narrowed his eyes as he watched for more muzzle flash, or the light of the sun glinting off the scope. Gut instinct said this was a different shooter than whoever had been after them in the woods. Their assailant had missed shots closer than one hundred yards. This man had nearly hit his mark from a thousand yards. Not the same man who'd shot at him earlier.

He assumed. He didn't think Kate had been hit, but...

He didn't know.

They were inside now and Micah waited, silently daring the man to shoot again, give away his position. Let Micah get his hands on him.

But nothing. Silence reigned in the wake of the peace-shattering shots. He made a mental note of the location he'd seen the flash—he would ask Noah if an officer was available to go with him for backup to check it out after he confirmed that Kate was okay and no bystanders had been harmed.

Micah turned, opened the shattered door and ran into the building. "Kate!" He looked left down the hallway. Empty, no signs of life. Turned right.

A door eased open. "She's in here." Noah stepped into the hallway, closing the door behind him. "Are you okay?" His voice was low, quiet. To keep his sister from hearing?

"I'm fine. I saw his sniper perch, or at least close to it."

"Where?"

"Bear Mountain, about a third of the way up, I think near where the rock outcropping is, the one we used to climb."

Noah nodded. "We'll go up there and check it out."

"And Kate?"

His friend shot him a glare. "She's staying here."

"Look, I get where you're coming from, but

if I'm wrong and I'm off even a little, you and I won't find his spot nearly as fast as Kate would."

"We can't compromise her safety."

"We're compromising it if we don't catch these guys." Micah stared at her brother. Glanced at the closed door, remembered how close she'd been to being shot, then nodded at his friend. "Okay, I see the point. We'll go alone. I need to call my boss in Anchorage to check in first and let him know to send someone to retrieve my partner's body."

Noah nodded and Micah stepped away, made his call and then walked back to Noah. He was about to ask to see Kate when Noah spoke up.

"All right, she's with one of my officers, and she knows not to leave that room until I get back. Let's go. On the way you can fill me in on why someone is after my sister and what this has to do with the case you've been working." Noah started down the hallway.

He noticed Micah wasn't following and turned. "You ready now? Or…" His voice trailed off and his eyebrows raised. The unspoken questions echoed in the quiet.

Micah stared at the door for another second, wondered why he needed so badly to see for himself that she was okay. Noah was the definition of *overprotective*. If she'd had so much as a scratch, he would have said something to Micah, would have noticed it. She didn't need Micah.

That was the truth, something he needed to let settle deeper into his mind. She didn't need him, never had. Even if he walked away right now and left her without his help, she'd likely be safe. Her brothers, the town, they'd all rally around her and no one would let anything happen to her if it was in their power to do so.

The uncomfortable element to the truth Micah felt in his heart was that…maybe he needed her.

And he couldn't afford to feel that way, even professionally, on this case. He was a trained officer. She wasn't. He should be able to walk away.

Where was that detachment he'd been so sure he could just summon up earlier? Seemed like he might have left that back on Hope Mountain somewhere.

And Micah wasn't sure if he wanted it back. But he needed it.

He turned away from the closed door, swallowed hard and walked away. "Yeah. I'm ready."

Micah just hoped it was true.

SEVEN

Micah's calves burned as they approached the spot on the mountain where he'd seen the sniper. His pulse throbbed in his injured arm. First thing, when they got back to town, he needed to have someone look at it. He knew better than to ignore a wound like this, but he hadn't had the chance to take proper care of it yet. Hopefully Kate's first aid would be enough for now, because he couldn't afford to be sidelined for an infection or anything like it.

"What do you think? Go up the west route?" Noah, up ahead of him, nodded at the cliffs.

Micah turned, looked back down at the town and tried to think in reverse of where he'd seen the flash. The west route around and up onto the rock ledge should get them there. If he remembered correctly, there were several shelves of rocks on this face that would make an ideal place for a sniper to nest.

He took the rocks faster than seemed wise, but

Noah was up ahead of him and he didn't like the idea of his friend finding something first. This had been his case for so many months and he'd already been invested in the outcome. The death of his friend and partner intensified that to an extreme degree.

Noah was making his way across the first rock ledge, bending to look into the crevasses that would be large enough for a man to hide in. Micah headed up to the next outcropping and moved across the rock, gripping the rough, cold surface with his hands. He should have had gloves with him, he knew better from his time living in Moose Haven. Apparently he'd been focused on work for too long, without enough time to get out into the mountains like he'd used to love to do. He was getting rusty. And while it hadn't mattered in Anchorage, his lack of skills here could be the difference between success and failure.

He set his left foot firm against the rock, bounced to test his grip, then reached up with his right arm to get a good handhold. There was a large break in the rocks just above him, and this was the only access. A sniper would have had to use a sling to carry his weapon on his back to get up to this perch, which made it less likely than some other places, but still worth checking out. He pulled his body weight up, tried to use his legs to push up as much as possible so as not to injure his arm even more and found himself face-to-face with sightless eyes.

Dead. Judging by the lack of decomp, not for long. He was looking at their sniper.

And it was Jared Delaney. One of the men he'd been after.

"Noah!" He called for his friend, pulled himself the rest of the way up onto the ledge, to the side of the body. As he did so, he noticed the red staining the back of Jared's head, the crimson pool on the rock. Single gunshot wound. Execution style.

He felt for a pulse on the wrist, knowing he wouldn't find one, but protocol was just that. He waited a few seconds but there were no signs of life. As he'd suspected. His own heartbeat quickened, and he looked around, down at the rock face and to the surrounding woods.

One rifle lay next to the body, a sling attached, as he'd guessed. No signs of other weapons, no handgun, so it wasn't a possible suicide. Micah looked at the body again. Not a surprise, because the angle of the shot would have been nearly impossible unless he was killed by a second person.

"I've got a body."

Jared Delaney was dead, shot by someone else. Almost certainly not his brother. Micah had delved deep into this history—too deep for own liking, with some of the things he'd learned—

but whatever the Delaneys were, they were loyal to each other. Christopher would never kill his sibling.

So he was right, there was at least one other member of this group, and it was more likely someone who was in charge. Unless one of the Delaneys' henchmen had gotten bold and killed his boss. He glanced again at the body. He doubted it. Forensic evidence would prove him right or wrong eventually, but gut instinct said this was someone who had more of a say in the operations than even Jared or Christopher. The man who picked their targets? Or who orchestrated the entire operation? Micah didn't know enough yet to speculate further.

"You'll want to come up a bit more toward the east unless you want to be face-to-face with him," Micah told Noah.

The other man didn't take long to climb the rocks, reminding Micah yet again that he was the one who was out of wilderness practice. The Dawsons were as good at it as ever.

"Is this one of the guys you came here to arrest?"

"Yeah."

"Looks like that isn't going to happen." Noah bent down and examined the scene much like Micah had a minute ago. Micah smiled at how familiar this seemed, how natural it seemed to be investigating with him. What would it have been like if he'd stayed in Moose Haven? Would Micah even have gone into police work as planned, or would he have ended up doing something else entirely?

Too late now to know. All he could do was move forward, try to make the right choice from now on. When this case was wrapped up, hopefully Noah wouldn't mind keeping in touch.

First, though, he had to solve the case.

"What's your take?" he asked Noah, already having made up his mind that his working theory had a lot of merit, but wanting to know if he was only seeing what he wanted to see.

"Someone didn't want him shooting at us."

"Someone on our side."

Noah bent down. Stared at the scene like he was listening for what it was saying. Shook his head. "I don't think so. Not with a single shot to the head like that. Average people shoot for center mass. A head shot… That's a little more personal. And usually a dominant sort of gesture."

He agreed with him.

Noah looked up. "What about you?"

"I think I've been assuming the Delaneys were in charge and that was a mistake that cost my partner his life."

"You can't take that on you, man. You didn't pull the trigger."

Noah was right, Micah knew it, but it still stung that they'd been outmanned and outgunned, that both deaths could have been prevented if they'd understood what they were getting into, the levels of this organization that they hadn't known about.

"I know," he muttered. "You going to call this in? I'm assuming we'll stay until your crime-scene team gets here."

Noah laughed. "This is Moose Haven. Crime-scene team?" He shook his head. "I can do some of it, and I've got officers who are trained in some of it, but if we get a scene like this, we usually get the crime lab in Anchorage to send a team down."

"Well, since this is your town, I'm happy for you to call whoever you need to call. I don't want to step on toes."

"We're friends, Micah. You're good."

"Okay, then call whoever needs to be called, but I need this body sent to Anchorage and for a forensics team to examine it."

"You want the evidence sent to state like we usually do or do you want it? It's your case, I can call APD if you'd rather, since you've been investigating the crimes."

"The state is fine," Micah assured him. "I just need this handled fast so make sure they know it needs to be high priority." He could hope that would work, but the truth was labs like that were overloaded. He knew it could be a while before they got back to him on the physical evidence.

Or it could be quick. You just never knew.

"You need it fast so you can make arrests?"

Something underneath Noah's tone made Micah sense that any feelings he'd thought were secret might be obvious to Kate's older brother.

Not that he had *feelings*. Just…protective instincts.

Micah swallowed hard. Met Noah's eyes. "So I can make arrests."

Noah nodded, relaxing slightly.

"And make sure your sister stays safe."

Sidelined her. They'd sidelined her doing a search, and from listening to half the conversation—the officer in the room with her had been talking to someone on the phone—she figured they were on Bear Mountain, one of the mountains that towered over Moose Haven, which she knew better than her own reflection sometimes.

The officer's phone rang. He checked the screen. "Excuse me. I'll be right outside the door."

Okay, so he'd noticed her listening in the last time. She didn't blame him for wanting privacy, especially when he was leaving her in good hands, since Erynn was a trooper, even if she was off duty. Kate knew from watching her brother over the last few years that it wasn't uncommon for the Moose Haven Police Department and the troopers to work closely together.

Kate glanced over at Erynn, who looked as nervous at Kate felt. Kate had never seen her less than self-assured, so she doubted it was related to the case.

More than likely it was related to the men out risking their lives to track down a shooter.

"You've got a thing for my brother, don't you?" The words were out before she considered how good of an idea it was to speak them. But for years she and the entire town had watched them banter, watched the way they'd fit together so perfectly, and Kate hadn't been able to keep quiet anymore.

Erynn's eyes widened but Kate held up a hand. "Never mind—I shouldn't have said that. It's none of my business." She might be the kind of person who didn't pull punches, but she needed to remember that not everyone worked that way.

The door opened and the officer came back in. "That was Chief Dawson."

So strange to hear her brother referred to that way, though Kate knew he deserved the respect that went along with the job he did. "What did he say?"

"He and Officer Reed are securing a scene and I'm to keep you here until they get back."

"Seriously?" Kate glanced at the waterproof

sport watch on her wrist. "We've been here for an hour and a half already and they want you to keep me here longer?"

"Did you have a better plan?" Erynn seemed to have recovered from her surprise at Kate's question and regained her usually spunky disposition.

"I can't think of many plans that would be worse."

"Officer James?" Erynn looked at the man by the door. So that was his name. Kate made a mental note so she'd be able to actually address him personally if she needed to. "Could you arrange for someone to have some food sent in?"

He nodded. "Yes. I'll be right back."

He shut the door behind him again and Erynn met Kate's eyes. "To answer your question, yes. I won't pretend I don't, but it's a bad idea for more reasons than I have time to get into, so please don't say anything about it again."

Kate felt her eyes widen. She was used to addressing people pointedly but few people were able to be as direct back. "Okay. I apologize." She certainly wouldn't want someone pointing out her ridiculous and doomed-from-the-start attraction to Micah, so she should have kept her mouth shut and not put Erynn on the spot.

Erynn shrugged. "No harm done. As for the food, I realized you could probably use it since it's probably been a while since you've eaten."

"It has."

"Then we'll solve that problem. Now, while we sit here, what do you say we do a little work on this case?"

"I'm a private citizen, Erynn. Did you forget that part?" Kate shook her head.

"You're the victim of several crimes and you're not the kind of woman to sit around while someone else solves her problems. I know you're going to look into this, Kate, at every chance you get, and so does Micah. I could see it in his eyes. There, by the way, is another subject we aren't going to talk about right now, but suffice it to say that the way he looks at you is more than an officer wanting to protect someone."

Kate swallowed hard. The idea of that…of Micah maybe caring about her as anything more than an old friend…was almost scarier than someone shooting at her. It was dangerous to have anyone care about you that much. Love made people hurt, because love involved loss sometimes.

Love, she'd learned early on, just wasn't safe.

She blew out a breath. Erynn was right about one thing, though. Kate had no intentions of sitting on the sidelines. "Okay, let's talk about the case. How can I help? What did you have in mind?"

"Noah means well, you know. He only wants to keep you safe." Erynn looked more hesitant than she did a second ago, and Kate felt her shoulders tense.

"But you're going to let me help. Because you know that keeping me safe means solving this any way we can."

"You know what?" Erynn shook her head. "I can't do it. I was considering letting you assist. But all personal feelings aside, your brother has actually worked with the troopers and APD on this case without the slightest hint of turf war issues. I can't do it to him." She shook her head again, and Kate saw her shoulders had fallen. At least she felt bad about it.

"Erynn, please." Kate wasn't above begging, not right now. She turned in her chair to face the other woman, hoping she could manage to look persuasive enough to convince her to change her mind again.

"Listen, just…" Erynn tilted her head to the side, seemed to be considering something. "You've got to think like law enforcement, figure out what Micah can't do without you and make him need you."

"Make him need me?"

"For the investigation to move forward at the best rate possible, yes. Figure out what skills you have, what you have to offer. And make him need you."

Kate nodded, chin up. Make him need her. She

hadn't been able to show Micah years ago how much his friendship—just friendship, even, plain and simple—had meant to her. So how was she going to convince him he needed her now?

EIGHT

The light rain had started to fall about twenty minutes into their vigil over the dead man and the crime scene, and hadn't let up since. It puddled in the depressions in the rocks, ran through cracks and made everything around them slippery. Both he and Noah had started to move at about half their normal speed. The last thing they needed to deal with was an accident.

"Getting down is going to be exciting," Noah mumbled and Micah nodded his agreement. Temperatures were hovering just above freezing, and while this rock was warmer than the surrounding areas because of the sun—it was free of snow, while the forest floor around them still had patches—if the temperatures dropped much while it was wet they'd be stuck here or need climbing equipment to get down.

Micah didn't remember the last time he'd been hooked up to a harness, the last time he'd used a carabiner for anything other than a keychain.

It surprised him, again, to realize how much he'd missed using those skills, how much he wished he'd kept up with them when he'd moved. He hadn't needed to completely reinvent himself when he'd gone to Anchorage, hadn't meant to at all, but it was what he'd done when he'd given up the things that reminded him too much of Moose Haven.

And the girl whose eye he'd always wanted to catch.

"When we get back to town, I want to know what you know about all this." Noah motioned to Delaney's body, looked back up at Micah.

He nodded. "I agree."

"And we need to talk without my sister around."

Micah shifted in his seat on the rock, his back resting against one of the ledges. He probably couldn't be less comfortable if he tried.

He exhaled, looked over at Noah, who was studying him. "Listen, I'm not sure that's what needs to happen."

"She's not law enforcement, Micah."

But she could be. Micah didn't know where the thought came from, but it was true. She didn't have the training, and he'd never recommend she go off on her own pretending that she did, but she could be an asset to this investigation if they let her, in an unofficial capacity. Even on this afternoon, having her around right now would help them track whomever had shot this sniper; she might be able to find their entrance and exit path…

Why he hadn't thought of that until this moment, Micah didn't know, but now that he had, he wasn't willing to let it go without trying.

"She's not law enforcement," Micah backtracked, agreed with his friend. "But if she was up here right now, she might be able to tell us where the guy went."

"The guy who shot this guy, you mean? The *murderer* we are now looking for?"

Yeah, okay, so this was going worse than even Micah had anticipated. Micah said nothing. Noah had already made up his mind.

"I know you want my help with this investigation. But let me be straight with you. I'm going to be a lot more cooperative if you're not involving my sister."

Micah hesitated.

Noah spoke again. "She's been through a lot, Reed. In high school she and a guy she cared about got caught in an avalanche. She lived, he died. And she hasn't been the same…" He broke off, looked away then looked back at Micah. "Listen, I shouldn't be telling you this. It's not my story to tell. But she's more fragile than she looks. Every ounce of stubborn fight she gives you, remember that behind that something is broken. Don't make it worse." His friend leveled him with a glare.

Micah's mind was racing. It filled in some of the gaps in understanding Kate. Answered some questions and gave him others. Micah nodded slowly. He still didn't agree that keeping Kate out of the investigation was the best way to keep her safe, physically or emotionally, but he did understand what Noah was saying, was glad to know another piece of Kate, though he wished she'd been the one to trust him with the story. Hopefully his friend would take his nod as agreement and let this conversation go.

And later on, when Micah had a chance, he'd talk to Kate, see what she thought about helping.

Not long after, several officers from the Moose Haven Police Department and Trooper Marks—the second of two troopers in Moose Haven—arrived. "I need to stay and help them, but you're welcome to go back—" Noah waited a beat, then continued "—whichever you prefer."

"I'll go ahead and call APD and arrange for a couple of our crime-scene techs or guys from the state lab to be sent down here."

Noah nodded.

"For now I'll go back into town, make some calls and try to chase a few leads." He tried to sound casual, come up with anything to say that was true but also wasn't *I'm going to go into town and kill time until you're done here and then bring your sister back to help me track where the killer went.*

"Sounds good."

Micah was careful as he made his way down the rocks, which were slippery but not as bad as they could have been. Kept his eyes open the rest of the way to town in case he was able to see any details that could help them, but as he'd feared he didn't notice anything. First thing he'd do when this case was over was take some personal time and take some wilderness courses. Just because it was the first time in all his years with the police department that he'd been asked to use skills he didn't have in an investigation didn't mean it wouldn't happen again.

He'd learned his lesson this time. Next time he'd be even more ready.

On the trail back there was ice, but it was obvious and Micah was able to choose his steps carefully. He slipped once but caught himself and slowed down after that, reminding himself he couldn't do Kate any good if he was hurt. The fact that his arm was injured was bad enough, but at least it hadn't slowed him down so far and Micah had no intentions of letting it do that at all.

Make him need you. Erynn's words had kept echoing in Kate's mind as she waited for the guys to return. She heard them over and over in her mind, rolled them around and considered how she could accomplish that—if she even could.

And wondered how much of a good idea it was to try.

The door opened, just over three and a half hours after they'd entered, and it was Micah.

Kate smiled, tamped it down quickly because she realized she probably shouldn't be reacting so dramatically to his presence. Not that a smile was dramatic. Maybe she was trying too hard to be cool, which would also raise suspicions.

She smiled hesitantly.

"You okay?" He looked to her first, not Erynn, not Officer James.

"Bored stiff."

"Want to come hang out with me for a while?"

She raised her eyebrows.

"Come on, Kate." He moved toward her, close enough to touch her, though he didn't, and looked down, the gap between them narrowing to almost nothing as he did so.

Surely it was unrelated that she was having trouble taking full, deep breaths. The man couldn't affect her this much, could he?

But she knew the answer already. He'd always affected her like this; she'd just been too young to be forced to admit her feelings for him were as strong as they were. Micah made her feel strong and at the same time like he was strong enough for her to lean on if ever she needed to. He made her feel brave but also like she didn't have to be.

He complemented her weaknesses.

And he was achingly out of her reach, even as he stood right in front of her. Because she couldn't risk her heart again, even if he felt the same. And she had no reason to believe that he did.

"Come on? What do you mean?" Was that her voice? The one that was soft, like she couldn't get enough air to speak in her full voice.

"I thought we'd already talked about this? Us not fighting. We were friends once, Kate. Can't we be friends again?"

Could they? Kate swallowed hard. Suddenly she wasn't so sure she had the answer to that question.

Behind Micah, Erynn cleared her throat. Loudly. "We are still here."

Micah stepped back, just slightly, and not quickly, like he had nothing to be embarrassed about at all. Like they hadn't just had some kind of moment.

"I know. I needed to talk to Kate." He glanced back at her, then looked at the other two again. "Erynn, tell Noah that we went to Kate's house. She'll be fine but he can come by if he needs to see that for sure."

"You realize they already know where that is." Kate frowned at the man she'd just been starting to trust. Sure, she wanted to go to her house, had begged Noah for that very thing, but she didn't know how she felt about someone agreeing with her, letting her go back to what had just been an active crime scene a couple of days before.

"Yes."

"And you're willing to risk it anyway?"

Kate looked at Micah, needing to know for herself the answer for her question. Was he willing to risk her life? She'd known him once but didn't now, not really. Was the case worth so much to him that he'd sacrifice lives if necessary?

No. It didn't take long to be sure of that. If he didn't really think she'd be safe, if he wasn't so sure it would help, he'd never ask this of her.

Which meant no matter how she felt, she needed to go.

She followed him to his car, and gave him directions to her house. It was less than two miles from the police department, though it was on the other end of town, so they didn't have much time together. Still, Kate supposed she could have tried to make conversation, but she didn't. She wasn't sure she wanted to hear what they had or hadn't found on the mountain. Now that they were back in town, the calm steadiness she'd felt in the backcountry had dissipated and she felt unsettled. She hated feeling that way, like she was weak, but it wasn't easy to shake when it came. It was better to just go along with whatever he had planned, hope she was up for it.

Because Kate wasn't weak, and she wasn't a quitter.

Which was why when Micah finally pulled into her driveway and asked if she was ready, she nodded.

Even as everything inside her reminded her someone had been killed here. Death had breached her escape from the world, from the death she dealt with in her job.

And it made her mad. And terrified.

NINE

In another circumstance, seeing the place Kate called home would have been intriguing. Now it felt heavy, like he was the one responsible for her haven being destroyed.

The front door had been kicked in—he'd fix that and make it stronger than it had been before he let her anywhere near this place without another officer—and the entire place had been ransacked, much like her cabin. The scene rubbed him the same way. It still looked like they were after something, not just wreaking destruction. But Micah was well aware that could be intentional on their part, to throw the investigators off from the truth. He wasn't sure yet which it was, and he didn't like that Kate's life hung in the balance while he worked to find out. This job was infinitely easier to do when you didn't know the person you were trying to protect, it turned out.

Kate's house was fairly minimal, which didn't surprise him, but they'd still managed to make quite the mess. He needed to call some friends of his in Anchorage who specialized in crime-scene cleanup and see what they could do for Kate. He didn't want her trying to handle all of this herself when everything was over and he was back in Anchorage.

"What do you have that they want?" He turned to Kate as she stepped into the living room and studied the mess for the first time. He knew she'd seen it before she ran, but he was under the impression she hadn't paid much attention to the extent of it, or even been through the whole house. Her face had visibly paled and Micah winced at his bad timing. Yes, he'd had to remind himself to treat her more professionally. Detach a little. But he'd overcorrected and moved to calloused.

"What do I have? You think this is my fault?" Her face was more anger than sadness, mixed with a healthy dash of disbelief.

"I'm sorry, Kate. I was out of line. I wasn't thinking."

"If you mean you were wrong to imply that I caused this somehow, then you're right and you do owe me an apology." Her eyes flashed fire, like they always had when she was mad, and Micah wondered if she had any idea how attractive she was, how intimidating she would be to anyone who didn't have the backbone to face her.

He wondered for half a second if that was why

she was still single. He wouldn't be surprised. It
certainly made no sense to him otherwise, though
a part of him was glad. The idea of her belonging
to another man was…not his favorite.

Impersonal. He was supposed to be moving
more toward impersonal. Micah shook his head,
cleared his throat. Tried again.

"So…apology accepted?"

She glared at him, then surveyed the rest of the
room. "This is worse than I remembered."

"Not surprising."

"No." Another annoyed glance that Micah realized he probably deserved. "It really is worse.
It's not my perception of it. I didn't get a chance
to pay too much attention, but I would have noticed if it was *this* bad. They came back."

"Before or after they killed the man whose
blood your brother found here, I wonder…"
Micah stepped closer to her. Protectively. "Are
you up for seeing the rest of the house?"

"If you weren't sure then why did you bring
me here?"

"Because I need to see it for my investigation
and I'm not inclined to let you out of my sight
while someone wants you dead."

"You don't trust Trooper Cooper or Officer
James?"

"Sure, but they aren't me." He knew how he
sounded, a bit like a Neanderthal, but the truth

was he didn't trust anyone to protect her quite the way he did, because to his knowledge no one felt about her the way he did. Even if he had no intention of acting on those feelings, which he'd done his best to keep buried for so many years already. He'd even dated some, in Anchorage, but hadn't found anyone who compared to her memory. And besides, he'd been focused on his career. It had been a valid substitute for the rest of the things in life he'd dreamed of. Like someone to fall in love with. Maybe a family.

"You left me earlier."

"Didn't have much of a choice."

She studied him for a minute. Nodded. Micah had no idea what she saw or thought she saw, but he was glad that for the moment she'd decided to trust him.

His phone rang, startling him and ruining the few seconds of peace between them. "Hold on. I have to answer this. Officer Reed speaking."

"Reed, it's Captain Clark. I just got your message. Officer Searls is dead?"

"Yes, sir. We were shot at when we attempted to arrest the Delaneys. There were more men than we'd counted on. We were ambushed." His partner had never had a chance. Neither of them had, really, so why Micah was still standing was a mystery he'd be working through for a while.

"Send me the coordinates and I'll send people for him today."

"Yes, sir." Micah knew his lack of rest last night hadn't just been because he was on edge, wanting to help keep Kate safe. There was also something wrong with relaxing into sleep while his partner lay dead on the melting snow somewhere in these woods. He swallowed hard against the bulge of bitter regret. That he hadn't been able to stop it. That he'd somehow been able to live when his partner was the better man by far. Stephen Searls had worked his way up in the police department after having grown up on the wrong side of the tracks in California. He'd moved here just out of high school, made his own way and been a good man. The first in his family to make good choices. He hadn't deserved to die.

"I'll finish this case, sir." He spoke again to the captain. He'd finish it well for his partner.

"I can move someone else on it if necessary. I'd rather not of course, because you know it inside and out."

"Searls and I both did." Micah took a breath, steadied his voice. "I can do this, sir."

"Good. Work with local law enforcement and the troopers—we don't want this turning into a jurisdiction mess. And keep me updated."

Micah ended the call, slid the phone back into its case on his belt.

"Your boss?" Kate was looking at him again, *really* looking at him the way she did when she was reading people. Micah nodded.

"I'm sorry about your partner. I don't know if I said anything earlier. But that's awful." Her tone had softened, along with her facial expression.

"I don't need your pity, Kate." Micah didn't know why it felt wrong to him, but he wanted her sparring with him like she had earlier, needed her at the top of her game to survive all of this, and for Kate that meant not being bogged down with emotions like the ones he was fighting. Regret, doubt and a bone-level sadness weren't helpful in working a case.

"And it's pity if I acknowledge that what you're going through is awful?" Kate shook her head. "But if one of my siblings said they were praying for you, *that* would be okay?" She shook her head, disgust on her features, and walked through a hallway to another room.

Micah hurried to catch up. He'd never intended to let her out of his sight in this place, because she was right. The killer knew where her home was, was familiar with it and would likely be back.

"First of all, I'm sorry. I'm not used to having someone be upset because I am." Micah shrugged, the uncomfortable truth rubbing him in ways he didn't appreciate. His parents had been big on pushing forward, using your ambitions to numb any pain you might encounter along the way to your goals. He knew their way wasn't how he wanted to do life—had figured that out quite a few years ago, but it was hard to break habits, retrain your brain to think a certain way.

"You're forgiven." But her words were brisk, her shoulders still tense. At their interaction, or at the underlying bitterness he'd felt when she said the word *praying*. She'd said earlier she'd stopped attending church, had some questions about God, but this felt further than she'd indicated. It felt almost hostile.

Help her, God. Help me. What kind of hurt did she go through to shake her so badly?

"Can we talk about that sometime? Why you don't go to church? Why you don't pray?"

Kate stopped, turned to him.

Micah waited.

Her heart, which had been calm while she was walking through her destroyed house, now beat a crazy rhythm in her chest.

No one had asked her those kinds of questions before. Most of the congregation of Moose Haven Community Church had kept reaching out to her when she stopped attending, after Drew had died. They'd given up eventually but no one had pressed her for reasons. Her siblings had never brought it up either, not directly. There were comments here and there about missing her at church, worrying about her, but nothing direct.

Why did Micah want to know badly enough to ask?

Kate didn't know. But if he cared so much that he would bother, she felt she should explain.

Later. Not now.

She swallowed hard. "It's a long story." Kate reminded herself to keep her voice even, stay in control. "Maybe another time?"

For a minute she thought he'd say no, press her again, but Micah was a gentleman. She should have known he'd be gracious. More than she deserved, maybe. The expression on his face eventually cleared, like the sky after a summer shower, and the tension all eased away.

She felt her own shoulders relax. Too much. She needed to keep her guard up.

Kate took a deep breath. "So where did they find the body—do you know?"

"You sure you want to know things like that? You have to live here when we're done, you know. Unless you were planning to move?"

She couldn't let herself even think of that possibility. She loved her town, the people in it, but what would it be like to feel like the world was open to you, that you could live anywhere you wanted?

With her search-and-rescue work, knowing

how understaffed this area was and how prone to danger with the mountain slopes, Kate couldn't just leave. She'd probably never be able to.

"I'm not moving. Where did they find him?"

"The upstairs hallway."

"Was he the one who trashed it?"

"We have to wait for forensics to answer that question."

Kate nodded. She should have known that, would have if she'd thought about it. Instead of saying anything else, she just started up the stairs.

"Wait for me, Kate."

She slowed, let Micah catch up.

When she reached the landing, she was glad he was behind her.

She'd seen death, more than once. But she wasn't used to seeing bloodstains on her hardwood floors, wasn't used to comprehending that they came from someone she'd known. She'd just been to Don's Mountain Store last week, getting her jacket repaired and picking up a new pair of crampons.

And now he was dead, his blood staining her house.

What had she done to cause these people to come after her? How could this have happened, and where did Don fit? Kate had no reference for dealing with this, wasn't very good at processing death anyway—she typically just shoved aside what she saw every day and hoped it didn't come back to haunt her. This murder was even more difficult to understand. Should she be sad about Don's death? Or had he been one of the ones chasing her? She didn't know why the killer might murder one of his own, but then again, the same thing had happened to the sniper. Was the man in charge of the group Micah was after eliminating hired hands?

"Was he one of them?" she asked Micah, desperate to have some questions answered. Any questions, really.

"We have to wait…"

"For forensics, I know. So much waiting. I'm kind of tired of it." Kate moved down the hall, only to feel hands grip her by the upper arms.

"Stop, Kate." Micah's tone was kind, as usual, but firm—expecting no arguments.

"Why?"

"Why would you go any closer?"

Kate didn't know. Maybe to see if she could find anything the police had missed, but when the thought occurred to her, she shrugged it off. She trusted her brother and he trusted his team. If there was anything to find, they'd find it.

"Fine. Let me get some clothes and we can go." She turned around, walked down the hall in the opposite way. Somehow, despite the mess downstairs, she'd expected to find her bedroom as she'd left it, but it was also destroyed. She hadn't made it upstairs when she'd been here and discovered the initial damage that had made her run.

Pillows were torn open, stuffing on the floor, drawers emptied of their contents.

"What were you looking for?" she murmured to herself.

"When we answer that, we'll be close to wrapping this case up, I think. They are targeting you, Kate, and since you didn't witness any crimes, the only logical connection I can make is that you have something of theirs."

"Impossible."

"What else?"

"I don't know—didn't we say it could have been something I saw? The avalanches last week that killed Gabriel Hernandez and Jay Twindley."

Micah seemed to be considering it and Kate was proud of herself. It was a solid theory.

"It's something we need to look into, but if that was all, they wouldn't have ransacked your house this way. There has to be more."

"I can't think of anything." She hadn't bought anything valuable lately that someone would want to steal, hadn't done anything exciting. "I mean, I take pictures of the rescue sites sometimes. You don't think…"

"There could be something on your memory

card that incriminates them." Micah wrapped her in a hug, releasing her as quickly as he'd gathered her in his arms, and smiled for the first time in too long. Kate almost smiled too.

"It's in my backpack, in your car."

Micah drove them there, and Kate was relieved to see that even if her house and cabin had been wrecked, her car was still in good condition, exactly as she'd left it. Because the Delaneys didn't know it was her car? Or because her theory that they were looking for something was wrong?

She dug in her bag, pulled out the camera, flipped through the pictures. Shook her head and handed the camera to Micah. "Nothing there that looks incriminating to me. If this has anything to do with my search-and-rescue work, I don't think it's because of a picture I took."

Micah looked through them and nodded.

She was about to ask him what they should do next when his phone rang. He motioned for her to climb back into his car and answered the call.

"Hello?"

Silence while the other person talked. Kate wished she could hear both halves of the conversation.

"So you're done? How long until you're back to town?" Micah asked. "Okay. That makes sense. Maybe we could meet up tonight for dinner?"

Another pause.

"Your sister is with me. Yes, I'll keep her safe." A glance at her here. "No I won't do anything stupid. Okay. 'Bye."

"Noah?" Kate asked, having figured it out mid-conversation.

Micah nodded.

"What is he done with?"

It took a few seconds for him to start to answer her and Kate wished she knew why. She was typically a pretty good judge of what people were thinking, but Micah had all shields up at the moment.

Almost one minute. Still no answer.

When he did speak, he was hesitant, would only barely meet her eyes. "Are you up for helping me with the case? I'd like your thoughts on the crime scene and the area that surrounds it."

He looked so serious, she felt so serious, for a second she just wanted to loosen them both up. The layers of heaviness seemed to have piled on them in this house and Kate was tired.

She raised her eyebrows. "Is it dangerous?"

Micah seemed to sense the tease in her voice, and smiled ever so slightly. "Extremely."

"But do you need me?" She smiled a little more.

"I do. Mostly, though, I need you alive. And if we have to take a couple of risks to get this crime

solved faster, make it possible to arrest those responsible, I think it's worth it."

The reminder of the stark reality that someone
was threatening her was more than Kate wanted
tonight. She'd enjoyed relaxing, just for a minute
or two, at the idea of Micah saying aloud that he
needed her. But she had to remember his words
were far from personal.

And that the stakes were life-or-death: hers.

TEN

"You know my brother will probably kill you himself and dump your body in the bay if he finds out you brought me out here." Kate grinned and Micah laughed, hardly able to believe the way she'd loosened up since they'd left town and headed back into the woods, to Bear Mountain. Today was much warmer than the day before, partly because of the winds that had blown through during the night. The Kenai Peninsula, while its own entity, was thought of by many in Anchorage as their personal Alaskan playground. It was surprising that this was the first case of his that had brought him down here.

"How about we just don't let him know about today?"

"If he asks I won't lie to him."

"I wouldn't ask you to." Micah shook his head. They'd just reconnected as friends and Micah knew it would be best for their working relationship to stay on good terms. Who knew when he'd be back down here in the Kenai for a case?

"Kate," he called.

She stopped and turned to him.

"You know I wouldn't bring you here if I didn't think it was necessary."

She nodded, her face reflecting the seriousness of his own, all signs of teasing gone. "I know."

"It's probably too dangerous. I probably shouldn't ask you to."

"I know."

Micah stepped closer to her, swallowed hard. If he'd thought she was attractive when they were younger, he hadn't had a clue of the woman she'd grow up to be. Short, so full of life and the bravest person he'd ever met.

Not to mention green eyes more vivid than Alaskan summer.

He had to stop letting her affect him like this. It was good he was able to think clearly enough, above his desire to protect her, to have asked her to come out into the woods with him to the mountainside sniper's perch, because he needed her help on this case. That's it. That, and to keep her safe.

After this was done, he didn't have room for her in his life. She belonged here, in Moose Haven, conducting the searches she seemed passionate about, doing what she loved. He didn't.

And he wouldn't ask her to leave that even if he did think he deserved her.

Which he did not.

"We'd better hike faster or it'll be dark before we get there," he said and it broke the tension between them, whatever this current was, just as he'd known it would. Emotions flickered on Kate's face for the fastest second and then they were gone again and she was back to the poker face he was used to. She nodded, turned around and kept going. If she was hurt at all by what had almost happened, by what he'd stopped from happening with his immediate refusal to step any closer, to pursue whatever it was he could feel between them, she didn't let on. But Kate never let things like that show. Not as long as he'd known her.

They slowed as the trail twisted uphill, toward the bare rock face where they'd discovered the body.

"Up here?" she asked and motioned toward the rock. He'd told her where they'd found it, described the scene the best he could on the drive over, but without giving her too many details. He wanted to know what she saw, not just as a tracker—although that was the main reason he'd asked for her help—but he also wanted to know what she thought in general.

"Yes, up a few feet and to the right. Let me

go first." Just in case. There was no way he was letting her walk into anything too dangerous, no matter how much he needed her help. The crime-scene team hadn't finished very long ago. He'd waited long enough to make sure they'd be off the trail too, and then they'd started hiking.

Micah climbed the rock in front of Kate, focusing on the cool of the rock beneath his hands, anything other than his unwelcome awareness of the woman in close behind him. The sooner he figured out who was behind this smuggling ring and gathered enough evidence to arrest him along with the surviving Delaney brother, the better.

He needed to get out of Moose Haven. This place made him want things he could never have, should never even desire.

"I think I found your crime scene. Judging by the stain on this rock." Kate's voice stayed even.

Micah climbed up behind her, stood beside her and nodded. "Yep, lying right there."

"And this was the sniper who was shooting at me, correct? One of the guys you were after earlier?"

"It was Jared Delaney. And yes, we believe he was the sniper. Haven't recovered any of the bullets that were shot at you to be able to prove it yet, but it's a safe assumption."

"Any chance he killed himself? Rather than get caught or something?"

Micah shook his head. "Not from the location and trajectory of the gunshot wound he suffered."

"Interesting. Any reason someone would want him dead?"

"I'm not aware of any. Criminals have enemies, but I was surprised to find him dead."

"Inside job?"

"Could have been. I can't really speculate until I hear back from the state forensics investigators. We're lucky they were already on the Kenai for a case so they could get here so fast."

"When will you hear back?"

"Depends on their caseload, but I'm not sitting around until I do."

"So you brought me here to help. What do you need me for?"

Surely he was imagining the slight smile at the end of her sentence, when she mentioned him needing her. Because yes, he did. But he certainly didn't want to think about it, would rather not admit it.

"I need you to crack something about this case for me. At this point, anything. Can you find me a trail? Something that might let us track him backward, see where he came from?"

"The dead guy or the one who shot him?"

"Either. Does it matter?"

Kate snorted, and he was pretty sure she rolled her eyes. "I don't track every person the same.

Different people make different choices when they're choosing trails and the more I know about someone, the better I can guess where they might go, then look there and possibly find evidence that my hunch was right."

"So it's not just observation." Micah hadn't realized that, but it made sense. The kind of skills she mentioned were used in other areas of police work and while none of them would convict at trial, they sometimes helped you know where to look, showed you a direction to go in.

"No, it's really its own art form."

"You sound like you love it."

"Tracking? I do." She was looking around the rock still, observing the scene.

"And rescue work too, I mean."

Kate shrugged. "I'm glad I can help people."

Micah opened his mouth to ask her to elaborate, but she held up a hand to stop him, then turned to her left and motioned with her head. "Someone came from that way."

"Which guy? Can you tell?"

"Maybe. How tall was your victim?"

He hadn't thought to look at the crime scene, but he knew the Delaney files forward and backward. "Five foot eleven."

"Interesting."

"So you're tracking…"

"Too soon to tell. But being aware that the

victim wasn't extremely tall may help a lot. I'll let you know." She started toward the trail she'd found, turned back to Micah. "Are you coming?"

He nodded, followed her into the dim of the forest.

It had been a while since she'd felt her heart pound with anything other than dread when she was conducting a search. This was new, using her skills to find someone who was almost certainly alive, but needed to be brought to justice. It took what she liked about helping people, but for once she didn't feel burned out, didn't feel like her gift was more of a curse.

She would have loved to follow her dream like Noah had, be law enforcement. But life had other ideas and she'd lost her right to make choices. Maybe not her right, but she'd lost the desire to. Search and rescue, avalanche rescue, was what she had to do.

A broken branch to her left caught her attention. The bush itself was only about three feet high—highbush cranberry, she was pretty sure, though it was hard to tell with the leaves gone and snow surrounding it. "He went this way. And judging by the broken branches, I think he went fast."

"You're thinking this is the trail the guy took

to get away from the crime scene, not the one he used to sneak up on the victim."

"Could be the same trail. But yes, you're getting the picture." Of course he was. Micah was one of the smartest people she'd ever known, something she'd always admired about him, one of the things that had come close to turning her starry-eyed as a teenager. He'd left town before she could make a fool of herself, thankfully, although she certainly was trying to make up for it by embarrassing herself now. What had that been earlier, looking in his eyes while he'd moved in closer, like there was…something between them? He'd probably been trying to keep quiet in the woods and she'd looked at him all wide-eyed like she was some kind of romance-novel heroine.

Good thing it had only lasted a couple seconds. And she hadn't done anything stupid like kiss him. *That* would be an embarrassment she'd never live down. She was his friend's sister, the current damsel-in-distress he needed to rescue. An old friend at best.

"Too bad the snow has mostly melted off the path," Micah mumbled and Kate smiled. Like she needed a fresh path of snow to track someone. All that would have done would be take away their advantage. She could track just as easily with the peripheral clues. She didn't need footprints.

She stopped where the woods thickened; the

piles of snow were more plentiful here. They might be able to see tracks in those, but if she'd been walking through here, hoping to escape detection, she would have been careful to put her feet on the parts of the forest floor that were either swept bare by the winds or iced over. She looked at the area for a minute, tried to think like the man she was tracking, then took careful steps through the woods.

She knew Micah was behind her, suspected that was the reason she was able to stay focused on her task without giving in to the fear creeping into the edges of her mind. Her siblings teased her on a regular basis about not being afraid of anything. It wasn't true. There were plenty of things she was afraid of; the backcountry just wasn't one of them.

Kate stole a glance behind her at Micah, just to feel her heart skip, just to see if it would again, and it did.

Yeah, there were definitely some things she was afraid of. She pushed on, deeper into the woods, mindful of the gathering darkness. She glanced at her watch. They had maybe thirty minutes of daylight left. Kate turned to Micah, bracing herself for the interaction so she didn't embarrass herself.

Again.

"We don't have much light left. Do you want

to keep going?" Kate hadn't decided what she'd pick if it was up to her. No, actually she had. She'd keep going, press through these woods till they figured out where this path led, who it led to, and then bring them to justice for the way they'd wrecked her life, ended at least two others that she knew of.

"I can't bring you out here again. Noah is going to find out."

"And kill you. Right. We discussed this. So keep going until we absolutely don't have a choice?"

Micah nodded slowly and she saw in his eyes the way he was questioning the entire plan, bringing her out here.

"Listen, I'm…" A noise made her stop, close her eyes and listen. She felt the cold wind on her face as the breeze picked up, even as she knew that what she'd heard hadn't been the wind. It was more than that too. She could feel it.

"Someone's here," she whispered to Micah.

"You see someone?"

She shook her head slowly, thankful that darkness had started falling quickly. Of course as soon as she thought that, felt the first bits of relief, they were cut short. Whoever was hunting her hadn't hesitated to come after her in the dark last time.

They were back on a mountain, a different one this time, and about to be in the same situation.

Kate had never had a panic attack, never really wavered in her belief that whatever happened was meant to be and worrying was pointless. But right now she could almost feel an invisible hand on her throat. Choking her air.

Could God stop this, if He wanted? Should she try praying after all those years of not reaching out to Him?

No, what kind of person was she if she was only willing to turn back to God because she needed something? What surprised her the most was that at this moment, she almost wished she still believed.

Did that mean that somewhere inside, she still did?

Kate fought down a swallow, looking around but seeing nothing out of the ordinary.

Fine, God, if You care, can you help? Something?

It was more than she'd expected to be able to say to Him, more than she'd meant to, and in all likelihood, it wouldn't do any good.

Just as fast as the sensation that they were being watched had come, it disappeared. Kate's shoulders relaxed, the tightness in her throat eased.

He was gone. Because she prayed, or was it only coincidence? She started moving toward where the noise had come from.

"Kate."

She ignored Micah behind her, driven forward by so much more than curiosity. She needed to solve this case, needed her life back.

"Kate, stop."

She didn't. She moved forward, through the trees easily and silently.

The woods grew thinner. Was that a clearing she could barely make out ahead of them? Kate stopped and gave Micah time to catch up.

"What were you thinking?"

"Whoever it is was gone. He…" She tilted her head and tried to search the darkness for anything that could help them. "I think he wanted us to know he was here and to follow him." Chills chased each other down her arms, down her spine, as she spoke aloud and she looked around. Still no sign of danger. Nothing obvious anyway.

"So you think it's a trap."

"I didn't say that—I think…" Something in the field caught her eye and in the dim light from the moon and its glow reflected from the snow it almost looked like a rock. Same color as one. But it was shiny?

"Micah, I think there's a gun in the clearing." She whispered the words, hoping she'd been loud enough for him to hear them over her heartbeat.

"Where?"

She reached her arm out, pointed her finger in

the direction of what she was growing more and more certain was a firearm.

Micah moved in front of her. "Stay behind me."

For once, she wasn't inclined to argue. The last ten minutes had thrown her off her axis. Why hadn't whomever she'd heard killed them when he had the chance, especially if he'd been in possession of a weapon? But rather than use it he'd dropped it for them to find.

And what about her desperate prayer? Did that fit into this somehow? Nothing made sense anymore.

Kate followed Micah, closer to what they'd seen.

It was a gun, a shiny revolver.

She looked up at Micah, able to see even in the dim light that his jaw was clenched tight and his expression stormy.

"What?" she asked, wondering if she wanted to know the answer to that or not.

"I've seen that gun before. I think it's the gun that killed my partner."

It was the last thing she'd have expected to hear and it rocked her. Nothing made sense. She couldn't get a read on the person who was after them, and that was rare in Kate's world.

She looked around, trying not to be too obvious in case they were being watched, but if anyone was there with them, she wanted to know about it…didn't she? She shivered.

Micah, who was too good at reading her for her own comfort, noticed nothing amiss. He seemed thrown off too.

"Should we keep going?" Kate was personally proud of how she kept her voice even and level, despite the way she felt.

Micah looked at her for a minute, something about the way his eyes met hers making her wonder if he saw through her more than she'd thought.

"No, I think we need to head down."

A shiver went down her back. She couldn't help but agree.

She'd had enough of feeling hunted.

ELEVEN

Micah's mind kept spinning around the facts, evidence and possibilities, trying to untangle them and form them into something worthwhile, something he could use to get some actual traction on this case. He'd snapped a few pictures of the gun with his cell phone, then placed the gun in an evidence bag he'd had in his backpack and put it in there. They'd heard no more signs of anyone on the trail and had given up tracking it to its end when Kate shut down.

Maybe it wasn't fair to describe it like that—she'd been strong and determined most of the late afternoon and even when darkness fell. But something about the near encounter had shaken her and Micah had decided that whatever they stood to find wasn't worth risking if she was so shaken.

To tell the truth, he was shaken too, he was able to admit to himself now that they could see Moose Haven in front of them, and were walking from the trailhead to his car.

"You need to go to the lodge."

"I told you, I'm not endangering my family. Or their livelihood."

And he didn't doubt Kate's determination, not in the slightest, but the fact was, something had him on edge too. Whoever they were after was unpredictable, but in a calculated way. There was a plan being acted out here, Micah was sure of that much, but it wasn't one he understood and that bothered him. That alone was enough to make him want more than just himself committed to keeping Kate safe. Her family's lodge was the best place for that. There would be plenty of people around, multiple law enforcement officers, including himself, her brother and her brother-in-law.

"What about one of the cabins? I saw on the website that Tyler has built a couple new ones near the lodge." That was the ideal situation in his opinion. They'd be close enough to get help but far enough away that if someone did come after Kate, it might not endanger her family or cause a stir.

It was better than going back to the crime scene that was her house. Micah hadn't had nearly the time he'd wanted to have to clear the place before he let either one of them sleep in it. Though the police had finished processing the scene, they weren't responsible for cleaning up the blood.

Kate didn't need to sleep in a house that still looked like an active crime scene, even if it technically wasn't anymore.

"I don't want anyone hurt because of me."

But she was wavering, as much as Kate ever did which wasn't much, but maybe enough that Micah could convince her this was the best idea. He heard it in her voice, the way it wasn't quite as solid as it usually was.

"No one is going to get hurt."

"You hope."

Micah didn't say anything else, didn't know what he could say. She was right that he couldn't offer her any guarantees, but really, would someone like Kate even want that anyway? Everything about the way she lived her life said the opposite, implied to him that she was willing to take chances, didn't want to know what the future held.

She'd always been that way, at least a little. Micah remembered her being at least as much of a risk taker as her two older brothers. But it was different now, somehow.

The question was… Why?

"This is the best option we have," Micah said and watched her reaction.

She nodded her head. "Okay. But I want whatever is farthest from the lodge."

It was more cooperation than he'd expected to get from her, so he would take it.

The drive to the lodge didn't take much time at all. Micah took it all in, amazed at how much it had changed in some ways—someone had clearly updated aspects of it to appeal to the changing tourism industry and had done a great job. But in other ways he might as well have driven back in time a couple of decades. More than ever he found himself wishing he'd kept up with Moose Haven, wondered what he'd missed all those years.

And wondered if one of the stories he'd missed was the one that explained the ways that Kate had changed.

"I'm not going inside the lodge." Kate's voice was steely, not a speck of emotion in it, just firm determination and Micah nodded.

"I know, Kate. I thought we'd call from here and ask Tyler if our plan is okay with him and if so, which cabin to go to."

She nodded, apparently satisfied. A woman he didn't know answered the phone and said she was Tyler's wife. Tyler was married? Once he thought about it, it didn't surprise him. Tyler was a good guy and was the marrying sort. He had a good job here at the lodge, Micah was guessing, and his wife would never have to worry about whether or not he'd come home alive at the end of a work day.

A privilege not everyone had.

"They said Cabin 3 would work." Micah turned to Kate. "The woman I talked to said Tyler would bring the key out."

Kate's brother came out the front door seconds later, jogging toward their car. Micah rolled down his window to take the key.

Tyler leveled him with a look not unlike the one Noah had given him. "Take care of my sister."

Micah nodded. Rolled the window up and then looked at Kate again.

"Ready?"

"I guess."

He pulled the car around to the back of the lodge, and followed the directions the woman—Emma, he thought her name was—had given him over the phone. She'd said this was the most isolated of their cabins and he believed it. Almost too isolated. He'd planned to stay in the cabin's living room with her in the bedroom—even if she didn't care about appearances he wanted it to be clear that he was treating her with respect. He'd also hoped to have another officer posted outside, in addition to Noah, who lived at the lodge. He just hadn't had the chance to talk to Noah about any of this yet.

Not that he was putting off calling his friend because he felt guilty about taking Kate to the crime scene.

But…yeah…

He couldn't delay any longer, though, because he needed to get the weapon sent off and besides, he'd never been one to run from his problems. At least not intentionally.

"Here it is." He pulled in front of a small cabin, more rustic than the other they'd passed on the way, but still not what he'd call roughing it. The brown log boards gleamed in the light from his headlights and he paused. Should he take Kate in now and clear the place with her present? He couldn't leave her in the vehicle; that part was obvious.

He might as well stop prolonging the inevitable. He shut off the car lights so they wouldn't draw any more attention than their pulling up had already done and pulled out his cell phone.

"Chief Dawson." Noah's confident greeting made Micah smile. His friend really did have everything he wanted here in Moose Haven, and the fact that he'd achieved it all before turning thirty-five impressed him.

"Noah, it's Micah. I could use a hand at the lodge if you're free. Or if you could send an officer."

"Everything okay?" His voice had grown tense.

"Yes, but I'm ready to get Kate settled and I don't have anyone to clear the cabin because I don't want to leave her in the car." Micah glanced backward, was surprised to see that Kate's eyebrows were raised but she didn't look angry. Only mildly amused. Well, fine, if she could find any amusement in this, better to just let her. She'd need a sense of humor to make it through this long haul.

"You convinced her to stay at the lodge?"

"Not at the lodge, but at one of the cabins. Number three. That was the best compromise we could work out, since I wasn't taking her back to her house."

"What do you mean taking her back? Erynn said you guys left the station and went to the house."

Micah didn't answer.

"You didn't."

"I did but with good reason. We're both fine—no need to panic now."

"Did I say I cared if you were both fine or did I seem like I was concerned for my sister? Listen, I know you're all hotshot, city police department now, but when a small town chief of police makes a request concerning his *sister*, it's a professional courtesy to do what he asked. Sit tight, I'm at the lodge and I'll be there in less than five minutes."

Noah hung up. Micah couldn't say he blamed him. He was actually a little relieved it was over with. Having things out in the open was always better than secrets.

He took another glance back at Kate. He had a feeling she'd disagree with that. But whatever secrets she held, she held tightly. He knew he was committed to keeping her safe; that much had been decided the moment he saw her in the woods. But he was going back to Anchorage as soon as he could, and while he'd like to keep in touch better this time with her and the rest of her family, they'd soon go back to being *former* friends. Almost strangers. It wasn't his place to know her secret.

"You're awfully quiet up here. Is my brother coming here to kill you?"

Micah couldn't stop the smallest chuckle at her tone. "He'd like to, I'm sure."

"I hope he doesn't."

And his uncooperative heart skipped a beat or two. He shook his head, hoping maybe to jar himself out of whatever dream world he couldn't afford to slip into and back to reality.

"Oh, yeah?"

"Yeah, because he'd be even more difficult to handle."

His heart returned to its regular rhythm and he shook his head again.

"Something wrong with your head or something?"

He looked back at her slight smile. Did she have a clue the way she affected him, how much he had to remind himself that she deserved better and he had no business getting to know her beyond friendship? Knowing Kate, probably not. She was confident, not one of those women who needed constant reassurance, but she seemed completely oblivious to how attractive she was.

"My head is just fine."

"Okay, if you're sure."

He'd missed this, their easygoing banter.

He'd come close to marriage once, with a woman he'd met when he pulled her over for a speeding ticket. Yeah, it was clichéd beyond all reason, but they'd laughed about that and he'd thought that maybe she could be the one. She didn't frustrate him at all, they never argued and it seemed like maybe…

She'd let him know about two weeks before he'd planned to propose that she couldn't see marrying a police officer. And told him that oh, yeah, she was actually already dating an accountant she'd met when she took her taxes in to be done in a new office.

They were officially over.

Since then he had never made it past a first date. Maybe because being a police officer was part of who he was, so he went ahead and made sure women understood that from the start. It turned out that while a lot were interested in dating a man in uniform, there weren't many who were actually interested in marrying one. While he knew Kate wouldn't look down on him because of the job, or discriminate against him because of it, he cared about her too much to give her a choice.

The job was rough on marriage, on families anyway. And that was true even for men who knew *how* to be part of a family. Micah hadn't had that growing up, not with parents as busy as his had been. He doubted whether or not he could figure it out on his own, and he wasn't willing to chance it with Kate, couldn't put her through both of them realizing he was bad at being a husband, maybe a father.

No question, giving her space, staying casual friends and not anything more was probably for the best.

But…surely it wouldn't hurt anything to be friendly with Kate the way he had been, tease each other with no expectation of anything else?

Micah needed sleep. Couldn't think anymore tonight.

The lights of a car pulling in behind him actually filled him with relief, the dressing-down he was about to get seeming worth it to pull his mind away from where it kept trying to go. And it would remind him that especially with over-protective brothers like she had, Kate Dawson truly was off-limits.

He was here to keep her safe. That was all, and to do so he had to keep his head in the game.

Because he couldn't fail at this.

Neither of them spoke while Noah checked out the cabin, to make sure no real-life boogey-men were hiding in the closet. Kate dearly hoped there weren't, because then they'd have to start at square one again, figuring out where she could stay, and she was so tired. She didn't remember the last time she'd needed sleep so badly.

Noah came back out of the cabin a few minutes after he entered, nodded at Micah.

"All right, let's go in."

She followed without comment, suddenly in-timidated by the current of…whatever that was she'd felt between them earlier when she'd been teasing. Micah had always been one of her favor-ite people to talk to because he could be funny, tease back and forth and then quietly listen to her, a fourteen-year-old, talk about how she felt lost in her family, in the midst of her successful, driven siblings. He'd never once laughed at her when it mattered, never made her feel less than.

She'd had the most ridiculous crush on him because of it once. And she needed to be careful she didn't go there again. Sleep would help. It had to if she was going to survive however long this case took to finish.

"You okay?" Micah asked her quietly as they walked the short distance to the cabin and he put his hand on her back to guide her in.

She nodded. No, she wasn't okay; she was confused and she hated being confused. But she was physically fine and decided that was enough to make her answer the truth, not have to go into it with him any further.

He was holding back too, must have his own reasons for that, and she needed to respect those, even if they'd gone unsaid.

Noah shut the door behind them when they were all inside.

"What were you both thinking?"

Kate widened her eyes. Somehow she'd been thinking Noah would be so happy she was fine that he'd ignore the fact that she was a human with her own mind and Micah hadn't dragged her to the crime scene without her consent.

Apparently no such luck.

"Before you get too upset…" Micah bent and started digging through his backpack, pulled out the gun in the crime-scene bag. Handed it to Noah once they'd all sat down.

"What is that and where did you find it?" Noah's big-brother voice was gone, the police-chief tone in its place. Kate had to smile a little. Annoying as he could be when he went into full overprotective mode, she did love her brother and she was proud of him and what he did.

"It was up past the crime scene. Kate was tracking one of the men through the woods, and we found this in a clearing."

"Just lying there?"

Micah nodded and Kate did too. She watched her brother meet both their eyes.

"I'm still angry."

A few beats went by.

He reached down for the bag the weapon was in, held it in his lap. "You think this is going to come back as a ballistic match for one of the guns we're already looking for?"

Micah nodded. "I don't have a single doubt."

"Then why give it to us?" Noah shook his head. "You said it was obvious? Not hidden in the grass, partially buried?"

"No." Kate spoke up this time. "It seemed like someone had left it there on purpose and wanted someone else to find it."

Noah muttered something under his breath. "Someone knew you were tracking him?"

Kate looked at Micah, waited for him to decide if they were going to tell Noah everything.

"We knew someone was aware of our presence, yes," Micah stated slowly. "We were already deep into the woods when Kate heard something."

The fear Noah had had for her earlier seemed to be back. "And you both kept going?"

They had, but not for long. Somehow Kate didn't think that clarifying that was going to help their case with Noah at all. At least not at the moment.

"He's messing with us," Noah muttered and Micah nodded. Kate looked at both men. They were each brave to a fault, almost. They weren't careless and she'd never seen either as the kind to back down from a fight, yet that's exactly what both of them looked like they wished they could do.

"I'm going to get settled into my room, if that's okay." She could listen there just as well and the two of them would feel freer to talk if they didn't think about the fact that Kate was listening.

"It's fine," Micah said.

Noah reached for her, gave her a brotherly squeeze. "Sleep well, okay? One of us will be awake all night. You just rest."

Kate glanced at Micah. "If you're going to let him stay up half the night, you need to get a nurse over here to take care of his arm."

"What happened to your arm?"

"Eh, little bit of a gunshot wound."

Kate rolled her eyes on her way out of the room. "Good night."

She walked into the room, which was already well lit since Noah had been inside checking everything out. She hadn't said anything to Micah, but this was one of her favorite cabins. The room she was in now had knotty pine floors—she knew because she'd helped Tyler put them in when he'd built this place—with a small rug at the foot of the bed covered by one of her favorite quilts, which had been handmade by their grandmother, as had many of those at the lodge. They were still in amazing shape, though, and luxuriously soft and warm, which was why Tyler had chosen to use them.

She sat at the foot of the bed, then leaned back to lie down, and listened.

"How is it possible to have a 'little bit' of a gunshot wound?"

"It could be a lot worse."

"I'll send one of the EMTs in town over here to look at it. You okay taking the first shift? May as well since you'll have to be awake for them to examine it."

"You're actually going to sleep?"

Noah snorted and Kate smiled. Exactly how she could have guessed he'd respond.

"This is going to last more than a day or two, man." Micah had lowered his voice, maybe anticipating that Kate would listen in, but she could still hear him and his words made her midsection feel old, like someone had dropped a chunk of glacier ice in it. Cold. Heavy.

"I can't sleep when someone is after my sister."

"Be smart. I'm going to sleep too, and I care about her safety also."

Silence. Oh, how badly Kate wished that instead of an exhausted person on a bed in the other room she could be a fly on the wall where the men were talking. Nothing was being said out loud but she had a feeling plenty was being discussed nonverbally. The silence felt weighty.

"You didn't seem to care much about her when you left and never came back." Now Noah's voice was the one that was lower, and not just in volume, pitch too. Kate would have smiled at her older brother's protectiveness—it tended to make him deepen his voice without realizing it—but she was too distracted by *what* he'd said. First of all, she'd never said a word to any of her siblings when Micah left, had never given the slightest indication that she was hurt he hadn't said goodbye or kept in touch.

Why would Noah suspect anything? And why, if he did, would he say something to Micah?

She swallowed hard, her heart feeling like it would beat out of her chest, a sensation that had become familiar during the last few days, except this time it wasn't for fear, at least not for her life. It was fear of an entirely different kind.

Please don't let Micah suspect I have a single feeling for him beyond friendship. Kate thought the words on instinct, wondered if she was praying even if she hadn't really expected to. And waited to hear what he'd say.

"I cared about her plenty." A few beats of silence. "And as her friend I care about her now."

"Her friend, huh?"

"You heard me."

"You seem awfully invested in her life, considering you just walked back into it."

Kate wasn't sure she'd breathed in the last thirty seconds. She was that focused on their words.

"I don't want anyone else's death on my conscience."

"Yeah, well, I want my sister safe."

"Then we agree."

Kate had heard all she cared to. It didn't go like this in movies. In a movie, she'd be lying here listening and Micah would say that it hadn't just been her with a silly crush that hadn't gone away. Had she completely imagined the few seconds earlier when she'd thought there was some kind of current between them, a spark?

Apparently. And she needed to remind herself of that the next time she got any ridiculous ideas in her head.

TWELVE

Micah's shoulder was freshly cleaned and bandaged by Noah's paramedic friend and now, at almost two in the morning, he was sitting in the corner of the cabin, watching. Waiting.

Noah had finally listened to reason and was taking a quick nap. Of course he wouldn't take the actual second bed in the cabin; he was on Kate's floor, insisting it was better that she not be left alone in the room at all.

Maybe he was right. Micah rubbed his eyes, blinked back some of his exhaustion and tried to sort through what had happened. When everything had gone wrong when he and Stephen tried to make the arrests, he'd known they'd gotten some case details wrong, namely who was in charge of the smuggling operation.

They'd also underestimated the Delaneys. As far as Micah had known, while they'd committed multiple felonies and would spend a substantial amount of time in jail, they'd not killed anyone before now.

Now his partner was a victim, as was Don Walters, the man the Moose Haven PD had found in Kate's house. They'd tried to kill both him and Kate. And she wondered if one of her avalanche fatalities she'd not been able to save was a victim of theirs also.

He should look into that more. Micah stood, walked to the chair at the small table by the cabin's kitchenette, unzipped his backpack and pulled out his small laptop. He'd thought to store it in a waterproof bag, one he had for kayaking, and it was a good thing since the backpack had been set in the snow so many times in the last few days' craziness.

He had just sat down when he heard footsteps. He jerked to attention, and relaxed when he realized it was Kate, walking into the main room of the cabin.

"Can't sleep?" he asked in a soft voice, hoping he wouldn't wake Noah.

She shook her head as she moved toward the couch. "Well, I did get a little sleep," she said as she sat down, folding her legs underneath her. He didn't know that he'd ever thought of Kate as graceful before, but she was. That, and confident.

"I'm glad for that." Micah reached to set the laptop on the table beside him. He'd already involved her too much in the case, and while it had been necessary and his decision had paid off, he didn't want to weigh her down with the reality of how her life had changed so suddenly any more than he absolutely had to.

"What were you about to do?" Kate nodded toward the laptop, perceptive as usual.

"Case stuff."

"Don't let me stop you."

He weighed his options. Noah was switching with him at four, so he still had two hours before he went to sleep again. He could work on it later.

Then again, the original sentiment he'd had was still valid. Didn't she still deserve to know how their investigation was progressing?

"We could just talk," he said instead of answering.

Kate laughed. "About?"

He couldn't think of anything, not in the middle of the night, not that would allow him to keep cultivating the distance he'd decided after his talk with Noah that he had to put between himself and Kate. Besides, he'd do well to remember the only reason they'd been reunited at all was because someone was after her. Staying focused on that would make her safer faster, and that was one of his biggest goals.

"Okay, I was going to look up some of the details of the avalanche you'd mentioned to me."

"With Gabriel Hernandez?"

Micah nodded, slid the laptop onto his lap and opened it up, looking up the news story about the avalanche online.

Kate shook her head. "You won't find much there. Avalanche stories are typically vague."

"Any reason why?"

"No, and I'm not sure it's even intentional. The press just tends to be gracious about not sharing details, whether out of respect for the family or what. You can generally count on knowing who was killed and where but speculation about the avalanche being human-caused or who was at fault is usually a nonissue."

"Interesting."

He looked over at Kate, but she didn't appear interested. In fact, she was looking away from him and her face had paled several shades in the last thirty seconds.

"You worried about what looking into Hernandez will trigger?" It was true that every time they made a step closer to finding out who wanted Kate dead, to who was the head of the ring of thieves he was after, something dangerous happened. Whether it explained her sudden hesitation or not, Micah didn't know.

She shook her head. "No."

"So what is it?"

"I'm tired, after all. Maybe I should head back

to bed and let you work." But her voice was wooden, mechanical, and Micah could see her going back into her shell. He didn't want that, a return to the person she'd been before she'd started to trust him ever so slightly as they ran through the woods together trying to evade a killer.

"Kate."

"Did you know Drew Redding when you lived here?"

Another friend of Kate's, one he'd always suspected liked her more than that. As in, part of the reason he'd decided his parents' move to Anchorage wasn't a bad idea. The Reddings had been in Moose Haven almost as long as the Dawsons, and were just as well established. They'd owned the grocery store, gone to church on Sundays and been the perfect complement to the Dawson family. When Drew and Kate had started getting closer as she entered high school, Micah had backed off. He had always known he wasn't even worthy of her friendship; she was that far out of his league, and he was probably too old for her besides.

"Yes" was all he said. "We didn't talk much since he was younger but I knew who he was."

She took a deep breath. "We were caught in an avalanche four winters after you left. I had just turned eighteen. He didn't make it." Kate paused, her face pale, breathing ragged. "I don't like avalanches."

Micah blinked, actually sat back like she'd hit him; the force of her words held that much impact. It wasn't her tone; that was unshakable, typical Kate. There was no feeling at all in what she said.

And if he knew Kate at all, he knew that meant there was too much feeling for her to even process. Push her any further and that facade would shatter.

He'd like to know the story. Understand why she seemed different now.

But at what cost?

He couldn't do that to her. "I'm sorry, Kate. I'm sorry it happened. I'm sorry I asked." He sat quietly, the computer on his lap all but forgotten. Where did they go from here? He couldn't ignore the words she'd said, but to follow up on them didn't seem right either. He'd give anything to go back five minutes and not ask at all.

We were caught in an avalanche two winters after you left.

We?

"You were caught too?" Micah winced as he asked it, hadn't meant to say anything more along the lines of this conversation.

Kate shrugged. Micah swallowed hard. When

she worked to avoid her feelings to *this* degree, he worried.

"Kate."

It was all he said, just her name, but he watched her face fall, her walls break. Her eyes were shiny with unshed tears that were so close to spilling over. First one, then another rolled down her cheek. In all the years they'd been friends as kids, he had never seen her cry. Not when her pet dog died when she was twelve, not when she'd broken her leg when she was ten. Never.

Micah, moved to the couch, held out his arms, desperate to do something to comfort her, wishing he could stop the torrent and knowing at the same time that she probably hadn't cried when all of it had happened. And she probably needed to.

She didn't accept his offer of a hug. He let his arms fall, settled for comforting her with words instead. "It's going to be okay." He meant it, believed it and hoped she did too.

She shook her head. "People say that but it isn't true."

"What do you mean? Life goes on, Kate."

"Not for him."

"But you can…"

"I triggered it."

He needed air. He was suffocating right here inside this cabin underneath the weight of a truth he'd never have guessed. He knew Kate well enough to know she wouldn't have done something like that on purpose; she meant she'd been the one to accidentally trigger the deadly slide of snow. But he also knew her well enough to understand that to her, the guilt was just as complete.

She'd not been able to save him.

Was that why she spent all her time trying to save other people's lives?

She'd resisted his arms when he'd offered them earlier, but he tried again now and she moved closer, tucking herself into his side, her head on his chest as she sobbed.

He held her tight, knowing that if Noah woke up he'd lose it, but not caring in the least. She needed him and Micah wasn't sure when Kate had needed anyone else before. The honor of that wasn't lost on him, though he wished for her sake he could take the pain away, even if it meant they'd never had this closeness.

Ten minutes or so later the crying stopped. She stilled, relaxed and her breathing evened out.

"It's going to be okay, Kate. One day, it really will be."

And he carried her back to her room, laid her on the bed and prayed she'd sleep through the night as he walked out and closed the door.

Kate had woken up in her room the next morning, so he must have carried her to bed because she had no recollection of getting there. He'd laid her on top of the sheets, put the quilt over her, and somehow as humiliated as she was by her uncharacteristic show of vulnerability, she appreciated that at least.

She'd all but shed her carefully crafted armor and had let him know the deepest hurts she'd experienced, the reason she stayed in Moose Haven, working for the search-and-rescue team. Even her siblings didn't know how the avalanche had affected her life choices after that, didn't have a clue that she still wished she'd had the chance Micah had—to leave town and go into law enforcement. If Micah hadn't already figured that out, she'd be surprised. He was good at connecting the dots— it's what made him an excellent officer.

Still, she hoped he didn't. And her siblings never would either. Because no one needed to know. Because in reality, her past hopes and dreams didn't mean anything. Drew was still dead. She'd been reminded of her part in that every time she'd passed his parents in the grocery store or on the sidewalk in town and they avoided her eyes. They'd finally moved last year, but her guilt hadn't gone with them. Their relocation hadn't changed the facts, hadn't changed how she felt about them. She'd still played a part in accidentally triggering the avalanche that had trapped her and killed him. And she still hadn't been able to save him.

Some mistakes couldn't be erased. Not by time or all the sorries in the world. Nothing could make him start breathing again, bring him back to life.

She closed her eyes, realized quickly that was not the way to escape from her thoughts and instead threw back the quilt that covered the bed. She'd have to tell Tyler that this cabin was every bit as wonderful as she'd always thought it would be. One day she'd come here on her honeymoon. Maybe. Assuming she ever found a man who didn't mind that she walked into danger for a living, that even if she felt the freedom to switch professions, she'd still choose a dangerous one since working in law enforcement had always been her dream. Before Drew. Before the avalanche.

Kate looked over to the dresser, then reached into her backpack for a fresh change of clothes. After she'd showered, she pulled them on, braided her hair and walked into the living room.

Noah and Micah were both sitting there, looking rough around the edges, like neither of them had showered. Her eyes stayed on Micah. His brown hair was mussed from lack of sleep, curling at the ends like it had when he was younger, just before he'd get a haircut. His brown eyes were warm. Fixed on her. He looked more hand-some than he ever had.

Kate looked away, cleared her throat. "So what's the plan for today?" Did her voice sound too cheery, like she was trying too hard?

"I'm about to head in to work. I got a call this morning from the state crime lab."

"Oh, yeah?" Kate glanced at Micah for a clue, wondering what the news was and if it helped them at all. "What did you find out?"

"Just what we already suspected. The blood-stain we tested matched Don Walters's DNA."

Kate fought a wave of dizzy nausea. "The one from my house?"

Noah nodded.

"So he is dead."

"Technically he'll be listed as a missing per-son. But it's likely that a body will never be re-covered. With the ocean right here there's a good chance someone…disposed of it and we won't see it again."

Kate shook her head. He'd always been a de-cent guy. She'd liked his store. It was strange to think of such a violent crime taking place in Moose Haven. It just wasn't that kind of town.

"Any other leads?"

"I had Officer James drive that handgun Micah found up to Anchorage last night so the crime techs could get started on processing it as soon as possible. I'm hoping to hear back on something today."

"Is their turnaround really that fast?" Kate asked.

Noah shrugged. "Not usually, but I called in a favor or two."

She could only hope it worked.

"Call me if you hear anything." Micah kept his voice even but Kate could tell how desperate he was for news. Good to know she wasn't the only one who couldn't wait for this to be over.

"You stay here and keep my sister safe." Noah all but growled the words as he headed toward the front door.

"Sitting still won't guarantee her safety, Noah."

Kate waited, stopped where she was at the edge of the room and let them continue their stare-down.

"Want to come to the police department with me?" Noah turned to Kate. She was impressed that her used-to-getting-his-way brother had even bothered to phrase it as a question.

She glanced at Micah. She had to keep a careful watch on emotions she wasn't used to feeling so strongly so she didn't humiliate herself further. But at the same time, it didn't feel right to separate from him. They'd been together for the last few days, the two of them against these faceless people who wanted her dead. She wanted to finish it with him, if at all possible. Besides, Micah was more likely to let her help.

Noah's version of "coming to the police department" with him probably involved shutting her in a windowless room.

"I'm okay with Micah. You focus on work."

Micah's eyebrows raised. So, yeah, he was supposed to be focused on work too. She knew that.

"Fine. Do what you think is best." Noah reached for the door, opened it slightly and turned back. "Be careful."

As he walked away, Kate moved to the couch. "It is strange that he let me stay with you without a fight?"

Micah shook his head. "He's understaffed. And he knows as well as I do that the police department isn't 100 percent safe. Besides, we talked last night, after you went to sleep."

Little did he know she'd been listening to that conversation. Although maybe not all of it, because she hadn't heard them discuss the case. She might have fallen asleep faster than she'd realized—not surprising since she had been several levels past exhausted.

"And Noah has agreed that taking you to some of the locations we consider points of interest in the case is more likely to yield results than either of us investigating alone. Whether you realize it or not, you have something they want. Maybe something we see when we investigate will trip your memory and give us a lead to follow up on. Otherwise, the case may go cold."

"Excuse me?" She hadn't considered the possibility the case might go unsolved until now. Kate couldn't live this way, not forever. For that matter, she was having trouble picturing living like this for another week.

"I won't let it." He said it while he stared straight into her eyes, and with everything in her she believed him.

Help me, God.

Another prayer. What was with her? Kate despised hypocritical people, those who turned away from God and then came running back in trouble. Besides, her life had been the opposite. She'd have faith. But when trouble had come, where had God been then?

She still had no answers. Probably never would. Something about being around Micah made praying feel like second nature, though. Whether he reminded her of her childhood belief or whether his faith was so strong it somehow affected those around him, she didn't know. But it was dangerous to her resolve to live life on her own. Trust no one but herself.

Now there were two directions in which she needed to be careful to keep the walls around her heart high. Micah. And God. Though it was getting harder to avoid letting her guard down with both of them. They both cared; she was sure of that, at least to some degree.

But she still had to be strong. Handle this alone.

Because neither one of them would be safe for her to trust with the deepest part of her.

THIRTEEN

Kate had gone quiet after he'd explained why Noah had gone along with Micah's plan to take her investigating with him. He'd almost asked if she'd rather not, but she'd already made her choice and didn't need to be second-guessed. Besides, he felt better with her where *he*, not just Noah, could keep an eye on her.

Especially after last night. He doubted her siblings knew how much the avalanche still affected her all these years later. Kate was a close-to-the-vest kind of person. Exhaustion was probably the only reason she'd shared anything with Micah last night.

Micah opened the cabin's front door, made certain the area was safe, as best he could tell, and started his car, then opened Kate's door.

"All right, all clear—let's go," he said from the doorway and locked it behind them. He noticed Kate had her backpack on, and he didn't blame her. Though the plan was to return here tonight, it was better for her to be prepared and ready to roll with any changes since they weren't the ones calling the shots right now. That was the biggest thing that needed to change today, in Micah's way of thinking. They needed something in the case to break, a way for them to be the ones with the advantage, something that had eluded them so far.

Help us, God.

"We're going to Don's store today," he told Kate on the drive; she was about as personable as a grizzly today. He understood, of course. But it didn't make it sting less that she regretted letting him into her life to the degree she had by telling him about the avalanche.

"And you think I'll be of some help?"

"I do."

"I'm a tracker. Not an investigator."

"Another thing we should talk about. You keep saying that, Kate, but you're asking good questions, better than a lot of people who aren't trained in law enforcement. You're observant. You should be using all your skills."

"I use the ones I need to."

"Okay." Micah saw Moose Haven's small downtown coming into view and knew it was now or never and that with Kate, it was better to shoot straight, see what she thought. "I'll just ask you. Have you thought about becoming an officer one day? A trooper, something? You need a break from just doing SAR work. I can see it in your eyes at the thought of anyone else being past the point of rescue."

"You don't know me anymore, okay, Micah? I said more than I should have last night, but it doesn't mean you know me."

She stared out the window the last half mile to the store. From the way she avoided his gaze, the tone of her voice, it was obvious to him that her words didn't hold the slightest amount of truth. And that he knew her much better than she would prefer.

"I'd like to do an initial walk-through and just get a sense of the whole place first."

"Was there some kind of crime committed here too?"

"Not that we know of. But we don't have any solid ideas yet for why the men I came here to arrest would want Don Walters killed, so we're looking for leads."

Kate grunted, or something that sounded like it. Micah kept his gaze sharp and focused as they walked from the car to the entrance of the store. He'd parked right in front of it, so he'd be able to see the vehicle the entire time, though he'd do a check of it before he let Kate climb back in, just in case someone had tampered with it. Thankfully the morning was quiet. Sunny. It felt more like he was in town on vacation than here on one of the most costly cases he'd ever worked.

But the task at hand was there and ready to remind him that wasn't the case. He had a job to do.

The store was typical of what someone would expect walking into a storefront in a tourist town in Alaska. Its interior was utilitarian and still somehow warm; the wood ceiling and the window displays made it look like a shop tourists would be comfortable in, with Alaskan-themed decorations and outdoorsy decor, even though most of what was sold there was very practical and catered to locals. Micah's parents hadn't spent much time in shops like this, but he remembered wandering in here once or twice as a young teen, mostly for espresso and to listen to Don's stories. The man had lived in Moose Haven practically since the town was started, and resided most of those years in an abandoned railroad caboose he'd turned into a cabin in the woods.

"It's hard to believe he's gone." Kate's words were barely louder than a whisper. Micah turned to her, decided watching her reactions might be even more important than keeping track of what his own were.

The question that bothered him the most was whether or not Don had been involved in smuggling. That could tip Micah off to whatever he was missing to lead him to who was behind this.

On the other hand, he disliked the idea of an older man he'd always liked belonging to such a group.

They had to find something with this case, though. So many leads and none of them had gone anywhere yet. Time was moving too slowly for his liking. As far as cases went, this one had delivered evidence faster than many others he'd worked, but it still wasn't good enough for Micah, not right now with Kate's life on the line.

"Did you buy anything from him lately?" Micah asked Kate as they wandered past the merchandise.

"From Don? How recently?"

So she did shop here. It was a tenuous connection at best, but he had to consider everything if he wanted to make progress.

"In the last month or so." The criminals who'd come after Kate had a reason for doing so at the particular time they did. Something had set them off. "It's possible he was helping the men I'm after smuggle artifacts."

"And what? There's something stashed in a backpack I bought?" Micah didn't blame her for the look of doubt she was giving him. It had been a long shot but sometimes you had to throw ideas against the wall, like he'd seen the Dawsons' mom do with spaghetti noodles when she cooked to see if they were done. Some ideas stuck, like the noodles, and some didn't.

It was messy work. But it was effective.

"Not necessarily. Just thinking out loud. There's a connection between the two of you… We know you have something the bad guys want and Don was at your house. Maybe he was there to get it back?"

"I don't think he'd have been involved in something like that. It rubs me wrong."

Micah had seen a lot that rubbed him wrong about humanity since he'd started doing police work but it didn't make any of it less true.

"Maybe not but it's worth investigating everything."

Kate nodded. Her expression remained unreadable and Micah kept a watchful eye as they moved around. While he seriously doubted whoever was after Kate would be lying in wait here, he couldn't afford to let his guard down.

Neither of them could.

Walking through the business of a man who had been found dead in your home days before was an experience unlike anything Kate was familiar with. The store was the same as it always had been, and while she considered herself to be a practical person who understood the reality of death better than most, Kate still half expected Don to walk in any moment. That he was gone was hard to process, at least in addition to everything else she'd been through in the past days.

The gleaming espresso machine—Don's pride and joy, since he'd opened the first commercial one in Moose Haven—still stood in the corner. The merchandise in the rest of the store appeared to remain undisturbed.

Don had made repairs to mountaineering gear his customers had bought in a small room in the back of the shop, which functioned as his office too. If he'd left anything behind that could explain his part in this, or prove his innocence which was Kate's preference, it would likely be there.

She started toward the back, not realizing how much she'd quickened her pace until Micah called after her.

"Wait for me, Kate."

She didn't want to wait for him. Didn't want to depend on him. With the light of morning, the realization of how much she'd told him made her want space. But she waited, then the two of them walked into the back room together. His proximity was enough to make her lightheaded.

Maybe she should have gone with Noah.

But no, this wasn't about some poetic attempt by the men to let her finish the case the way it had started—with Micah—as she'd so foolishly thought of earlier. It was a practical decision. She was here because she was supposed to be helping with observation. They were counting on her to notice things.

Think like a tracker, Kate. Not some woman who runs scared at the first sign of danger. Or gets distracted by a man, of all things.

"Were the police here? After Don was killed?"

Micah nodded. "The people from the state crime lab did a walk-through just to determine whether or not there was any evidence of wrongdoing on Don's part. They got a lot of papers out of his filing cabinets."

Kate nodded, looked around the room again.

"Did they take anything else?"

"Not that they mentioned, why?"

"Look around." Kate had taken a few seconds longer than she felt she should have to notice what was off about the back room, but it made her feel slightly better that Micah hadn't noticed yet either.

She watched him scan the room. Halfway through he stopped, looked at her.

"Where is everything he was altering? If this is a thriving business there should be something here."

"Exactly." Kate shivered and started moving around the stacks on Don's desk, in case anything there gave them a lead.

"I don't like it."

"The room? It's just weird because the man who used to use it is dead." At least, that's what she was telling herself. The unease was creeping around her consciousness at the edges too, but she knew if they left now, she wouldn't come back. She didn't want to miss a detail that could make a difference in this case, help the nightmare end sooner, just because she'd been scared. "No one thought his mail should be investigated?" She reached for the envelopes, which sat on top of a brown box on the desk. Her hand brushed the box as she did so.

"Stop. Don't move at all."

Micah's voice left no room for argument, arrested her motion before she'd finished processing what he'd said. Her hand rested on the box.

"What? Can I move my hand now?"

"No. Don't move."

Kate blinked. He was serious.

"That box doesn't have a return address."

"Okay…"

"Or anything indicating the postage."

Kate's eyes widened, remembering stories she'd seen in the news before, in places far enough away and in cities, where mail contained bombs or diseases.

And her hand was on it.

"What do I do?"

"We need to get out of here."

"I think that's a great idea, but my hand is still resting on top of what I assume you suspect is a bomb."

"Kate."

"Yes?"

"Do you trust me?"

Did she? She'd spent so many years trusting herself, but the way she'd behaved with Micah the last few days told the truth. She trusted him too. Her stomach jumped at the realization. She really did.

"Yes." It was barely above a whisper, her own disbelief preventing her from saying it any louder.

"Do exactly what I say."

She would, if it meant they would live. This was different than the other times her life had been threatened. This was slow motion, the ability to soak in every second of terror and wonder if it would be the last. No running, no obvious surge of adrenaline to help mitigate the feelings of fear.

Actual, real fear. It was so rare she felt it, that it shook Kate to her core. And it wasn't of dying. Wasn't that she was afraid of blowing up.

It was of the fact that once again she was completely powerless. Just like during the avalanche. Out of control.

"Okay."

"When I tell you to, let go and run as fast as

you can. Do not look back for me, don't do anything. Just. Run."

She nodded.

"Ready?"

Another nod.

"Now."

She jerked her hand from the box, hitting it against the stack of mail on top of it as she did, and ran, just like Micah had said. For about half a second before she realized she couldn't do it, she couldn't leave him there. She whirled around, back to the office, but ran into Micah's chest.

"I'm here. And I said run. Go!"

She kept running, stumbled over something in the path when she was almost to the door, only to have Micah take her hand and pull her forward.

They hadn't reached the door when the store exploded behind them.

Kate was back in slow motion.

A giant fist seemed to hit her in the back, her ears stabbing with pain she didn't understand. Then she was falling, her hand still in Micah's.

They hit the ground.

And after a couple seconds of having the wind knocked out of her, Kate took a long breath. She was alive. She glanced over at Micah—his eyes were closed.

Not again.

Please, God, not again.

* * *

Micah blinked his eyes open after the blast, conscious of the sound of the fire crackling in the background, the fire alarm of the shop blaring, aware of the fact that he'd done it, he'd gotten Kate far enough away that they should be okay. His muscles ached, and judging by the sharp pain in his arm he'd reopened the wound, but she was safe, and that was what mattered.

Thank You, God.

He sat up, glanced over at her. She was…crying?

"Kate?"

Her head whipped around. "You're okay?" She blinked her eyes, bright green with the tears, in disbelief as she spoke.

Micah nodded, watched her swallow hard and blink back the tears. He frowned, not able to see where she was hurt. "What's wrong? You're sure you're okay?" No physical injuries that he could see, but he knew that blast victims were often injured most internally.

"I'm fine," she sniffed. "You're fine?"

He nodded.

"Let's get out of here." Kate pushed herself up off the ground.

"I need to get the police here." Micah stood, looked around and dialed Noah's number to explain the situation. The blast had set off a fire in the back room; some of the clothes racks had been knocked over and the glass had been broken in the front of the store. Thankfully it had shattered into the empty sidewalk and not toward them. "I'm not taking you outside right now."

"The building we are in is on fire and potentially unstable," Kate argued.

Micah was already shaking his head. "And whoever is after you could be sitting outside waiting to take you out if the explosive device didn't succeed."

She stopped arguing with him after that. He hated that he'd had to scare her, but he didn't know what to do with Kate when she behaved like this. Like…well, not herself.

Noah and the rest of the Moose Haven officers on duty arrived minutes later. Noah stalked toward Micah, his face set in a scowl. He could promise he'd seen the man smile when he was a kid, but it didn't seem to be something he did often. Or maybe it was only a problem when someone was after his sister. Micah wasn't sure.

"You told me you'd keep her safe."

"And she's safe."

"Find anything today?"

"Maybe. We noticed nothing was waiting for repairs in the back room, and no completed garments or gear was there either."

Noah nodded. "The crime-scene team also made a note of that."

So their investigation in the building had been for no reason. He'd risked her life again and had literally nothing to show for it.

He had to get out of here.

"I've got to go to Anchorage. I need to talk to my boss in person." He had unreturned messages from the chief on his phone, not to mention the fact that he wanted to get his hands onto the files in his desk, the handwritten pages of notes from when he and Stephen had been working this case. He'd missed something—*they* had missed something. And he needed to look at his notes to figure out what it was.

"Take Kate with you."

"What?" He'd expected a lot of things from Noah after the way this morning had gone. That wasn't one of them.

"She needs to get out of Moose Haven while we try to figure this out. If I could find a way to keep her out of town for longer, till we're done, I'd do it in a heartbeat."

"I'm only planning to be there for the day. Maybe one night."

"Good enough. You work the case from there, let me work it from here and keep her out of it."

Micah could see where Noah was coming from. The people who were chasing him and Kate did want her out of the picture, but it wasn't likely they'd leave Moose Haven to go after her, not if they were still working on any aspects of their illegal "business" from near Moose Haven. Of course there was always a risk. But a change in location could help.

"Did I hear my name?" Kate walked over.

"The EMTs finished checking you out?" Micah asked before he filled her in on any of the potential plans. He looked at her face, still assessing to make sure no one had missed anything. If she'd been hurt… His heart couldn't take thinking about it, not when she'd just reentered his life. He was already asking himself how he'd been without her for so long, wondering how he'd return to living life without her when the case was over. He must have stared a second too long because he felt her watching him. Looked away. But not before Noah caught his gaze, his eyebrows rising like a knowing brother's. Micah might be able to keep his feelings from Kate, but her brother wasn't ignorant of them. Not in the least.

Kate looked good physically, but he wished he knew how she was feeling inside about all this. That wasn't something he could assess with just a look. He'd felt the fear radiating from her in the office just before the bomb went off, wanted to talk to her about it, but knew this wasn't the time. Not with her brother listening. He understood, after watching how Noah handled situations, why Kate would feel the need to prove herself so capable and immovable.

"They did and they said I'm fine. Which I told you earlier." At least she was back to her slightly sarcastic self. It was better than the odd, quiet way she'd looked at him in the initial moments following the explosion.

"Glad to hear it. I'm going to go ask them to look at my arm, but after that, want to go for a road trip?" Micah tried his best to keep his voice light, but was still replaying the scene from earlier in his head over and over, seeing her hand on that box, gut instinct telling him it was a bomb and he may finally have let her walk right into a situation that she wasn't going to be able to walk out of.

She looked over at Noah. "You think my brother will let me out of his sight after this morning?"

"I think it's a good idea."

She looked back at Micah. Nodded. "Okay. I'll get my backpack."

FOURTEEN

Micah hadn't said much since they left Moose Haven and got on the Seward Highway, which would take them off the Kenai Peninsula and up to Anchorage. She didn't know if he was preoccupied with the case or upset with how she'd handled the situation earlier. She'd run it over in her mind multiple times and there were so many things she should have done better. She'd let her guard down, something she should have learned by now not to do.

And both of them had almost gotten killed.

She couldn't handle anyone else dying when she could stop it. Especially not Micah. She cared about him more than was safe for her heart, but she couldn't keep denying it, at least not to herself.

"You sure you're all right over there?"

He finally spoke when they'd just crossed the tall bridge over Canyon Creek, well on their way north. Kate tore her eyes from the scenery out the window and looked over at him. "It's been a long couple of days."

"It has."

"Why did you want me to come with you?"

"Noah thought…"

"Not Noah. Why did you think I should come?" She'd heard what he'd said about her being able to pick up on details, maybe being able to help with the case, but so far it didn't feel to her like she had been able to do so. Was Micah still hoping she'd offer some help or was he just trying to keep her out of danger?

But maybe some part of her wondered if someone still thought…that if she had the choice, she could do this. The job Micah did every day. What Noah did.

"I still think we could use your help."

Her shoulders relaxed and some crazy flicker of hope sparked inside her.

"I want to help."

Micah glanced over at her and Kate swallowed hard. How was it the man heard the things she didn't say, was almost more in tune with feelings she didn't know how to articulate than she herself was?

It made no logical sense, and Kate disliked that. Life should be black-and-white. Clear.

The way Micah interacted with her, the way he made her feel, all of him was anything but.

"Kate?"

"Hmm?"

"Tell me more about the avalanche. The one you were in."

Of all the subjects he could have broached when they were trapped in a car-sized space together, this would have been the last one she'd have guessed he'd choose and the last she'd have wanted him to. Micah was a gentleman in all areas, didn't push, not even for answers or explanations. She'd told him all she wanted to last night.

And yet he was asking again.

"I told you most of it."

"You said it was your fault. But you didn't tell me why you think that."

"Why I *think* that?" Kate turned to him, the seat belt catching her back, she'd jerked around so fast. "I was there, Micah. I got caught in the snow. I'd heard but never dreamed it could wreak that kind of destructive power with so little warning. We had none of it. Nothing anyone says, the sound, the obvious conditions…it was winter in the backcountry and a freak slab released, caught us both and then somehow decided to spit me out and let me free while taking the life of my best friend. *I* was the one that wanted to go skiing that day. I was the one who picked the spot. I was the one who said *just one more run*. And if I hadn't done any of those things? He'd still be alive."

"You loved him, didn't you?"

"I was eighteen. I don't know. But I wish I'd had the chance to find out."

He said nothing, just gave her a quiet space for her words to land as the car kept bringing them forward, toward Anchorage. Kate avoided the city when she could. It reminded her of too many things she could never have, of too many opportunities she needed to ignore.

Of the standing invitation she had from a man she'd rescued once, a man who worked with the troopers and had encouraged her to apply.

She'd avoided Anchorage like the plague ever since, not sure she was strong enough to resist the temptation of having everything she wanted so close within her reach without being able to do anything about it. She owed it to Drew to make the backcountry safer for people, to be around to save those who made bad choices like she had that day. It was why she'd chosen search-and-rescue work. Or rather, why it seemed like it had chosen her.

"It wasn't your fault, Kate."

"Stop it. I've heard all this before."

Unlike everyone else, he stopped. Kate was grateful for the quiet for the first ten minutes and then the shadow of her past, and her other familiar companion, guilt, rested on her like a weight she couldn't shake off.

And she wished he'd say anything.

But instead he was quiet, just like she'd wanted. She'd pushed him away over and over and he'd finally listened.

And there was nothing she could do to go back and change his mind.

They pulled into the gated parking lot at the Anchorage Police Department on a gorgeous sunny day. It was funny how the traffic Micah had been so used to seemed unreasonable this morning. Small-town living had gotten back in his blood fast, but he'd have to remember it was temporary. He'd solve this case soon—he was hoping it was a matter of days now.

He'd tried rekindling his friendship with Kate, but it was clear she didn't want that. He wasn't in the habit of forcing things that other people didn't want, and it was time to start respecting the lines she'd drawn so clearly in the Moose Haven dirt.

"You ready?" she asked him now, the first she'd spoken in well over an hour.

"For this?" He was, more than he could say. Something about being back here, seeing the building where they'd made so much progress in the case. "You have no idea."

"Pretty sure I have as much reason to want him

brought to justice as you." She smiled slightly, and he recognized a small truce when it was offered. He smiled back.

They walked into the building together, into the familiar entryway, then to the chief's office.

He knocked on the door.

"Come in," Chief Clark called and Micah motioned for Kate to go first. She did so without hesitation and he was struck again by her confidence. She wasn't arrogant; she stepped to the side as he entered and hadn't said anything yet.

The chief stood, stuck his hand out to Kate. "Chief Clark."

"I'm Kate Dawson. Nice to meet you, sir."

The chief glanced at Micah, then back at Kate. "You're the one who's being threatened?"

"I am."

"What's she doing here, Officer Reed?"

He swallowed hard, not sure why he hadn't anticipated the conversation taking this turn. "There was another threat against her life last night and this was the safest option."

"To bring her to our meeting? I have a room she can sit in while we talk."

She turned to Micah, stared him down with eyes that didn't flinch. They'd told her they wanted her help, and he did and Noah mostly did. The chief… Micah hadn't exactly run the plan by the chief, as he was fully aware of the protocol for involving non-officers in a case. Especially when the person in question was a victim. Especially when it was an attractive woman who might put his professionalism in question. Micah knew his motives and choices were good, but he wasn't the one who needed convincing.

"I'd be happy to go sit somewhere else. Wouldn't want to get too involved in your case."

He heard the dry irony in her words, doubted the chief did. They were respectful enough. Detached. And he had no choice but to follow through. So he didn't say anything, didn't contradict what his boss had requested.

"I'll have an officer sent in."

An officer Micah knew, but not well, entered a minute later and Kate followed him out, not turning to give him a second glance. Micah stared at the door as it closed.

"Something you need to talk to me about, Reed?"

He turned back to his boss, a fair man whom he respected, and tried to remind himself that it wasn't the chief's fault that he'd gotten himself all tangled back up with the Dawson family.

"Nothing inappropriate, sir."

"You seem extremely familiar with one of the victims in our case here."

"We were childhood friends, when I lived in Moose Haven."

"Did I know about your connection to the town?"

"I'm not sure if you did personally, but HR knew that, as it was part of the extensive background check I was given when I was hired ten years ago." Maybe the last part had been a little much, but he was tired of being treated with suspicion. He was doing his job and he was doing it well.

"No need to get defensive."

Wasn't there?

The chief spoke again. "Listen, before we get into details, let's cut to one of the main reasons I'm glad to see you in person today. I need to know if you can handle this, Reed. Do I need to take you off this case? It seems personal on several fronts."

Personal. The death knell of having responsibility for a case.

Micah took a breath, looked down at his hands and willed his heart rate to slow, his mind to settle.

"I don't need to be taken off the case. It's hard not to have a connection to anyone in a town that small, sir, but I assure you my relationship with Kate Dawson is strictly professional."

"Professional. So the reason she seems to be fairly involved in this case is…?"

"She's the best tracker in Moose Haven."

"I can send someone down if you need a tracker."

"They won't be as good as she is, sir. And that's an objective opinion. You're welcome to call the Moose Haven Police Department for a second opinion."

"No need. Besides, that wouldn't exactly be objective, would it? Since there's another Dawson who is the chief of that department?"

"I told you, small town."

The chief studied him for another minute, finally nodded and Micah could have sunk backward into the chair with relief, if that wouldn't have looked the antithesis of professionality. So he contented himself with exhaling a long breath.

"Let's talk about the case, then."

"At the moment I'm waiting for results of some of the evidence we've sent to the lab."

"And did I understand the message you left me earlier correctly? Someone tried to blow the two of you up?"

"Yes, sir."

"What's your take on this, Reed? Why does someone want Kate Dawson dead? Or do they not?"

The last question threw him for a loop, but

when he thought about it, it was a valid one. "I had been working under the assumption that she had something the criminals wanted."

"Evidence against them?"

"Or an artifact she came into possession of without knowing."

"Either is a possibility. And do you think that now?"

Micah shrugged a shoulder, turned his head. "It's possible. But I want to explore the possibility that someone wants her dead because of what she saw."

"And you think that is…"

"As I told you on the phone, two men, Gabriel Hernandez and Jay Twindley, were killed in avalanches in Moose Haven, days before she was attacked for the first time. I looked into Twindley and he's clear. Besides, my avalanche contact said the avalanche that killed him wasn't as suspicious as the one that killed Hernadez. I've been looking into him and I'm starting to think there's a good chance he was part of the organization. I've been investigating him the best I can from Moose Haven, looking into his background. He did a few years in prison at the same time as one of the Delaney brothers. There's a good chance he was involved."

"You have any more on the scope of it?"

"Not yet. Not as much as I'd like to. I still don't

know how Stephen and I missed that there were more people involved than we'd initially thought."

"Because whoever is in charge knows what they're doing."

"Unfortunately true, sir," Micah agreed.

"I'll have someone here look into his record more, see if they can get the state to rush Hernandez's autopsy results."

"There was an autopsy? I didn't think that was commonplace with avalanche victims."

The chief shrugged and kept talking. "Someone in his family had the thought to order one. A sister, I think, who didn't believe her brother would have been out in the kind of weather Moose Haven was having that day without being impaired somehow."

Micah raised his eyebrows. "And she wanted to prove that?" Seemed strange to him, but the chief just shook his head.

"People want answers, Reed. Sometimes it doesn't matter if they're the ones they wanted or not, at least they have their answers."

Micah started toward the door.

"Wait," the chief said. "One more thing. Looks like the victim's sister asked that you investigate a location she thought might have evidence about her brother's death. It's too shaky to get a warrant, so you won't be able to go inside, but if you wanted to go up there, see what you could see without violating any constitutional rights…"

"What's the location?"

"Chris Delaney's cabin."

"Did you say 'Chris'?" The cabin where he and Stephen had been ambushed had been in Jared Delaney's name. Was there a second cabin?

"That's what she said."

Thoughts chasing around in his head, Micah nodded, managed to say "thank you" and left the room.

He needed to talk to Noah, work out some details and ideas that were formulating in his mind.

And then he had a cabin to find.

FIFTEEN

For the second time in a week Kate was stuck in a room being bored while someone else was making actual progress on the case. It was maddening to her, and this time her babysitter wasn't as fun as Erynn Cooper and was far less likely to convince her she should talk Micah into thinking he *needed* her.

Had those words ever been a mistake to follow? She'd seen how that meeting with his boss had gone.

The door opened and she glanced up. It was Micah, but she was careful not to smile, or give any indication that she recognized him. Why hadn't she considered that as another reason she needed to get ahold on her ridiculous crush from ages ago? This could cost him his job, and she couldn't handle knowing she'd caused that.

"We did all we needed. Let's head out."

She stood, not bothering to say goodbye to the officer who hadn't offered much conversation anyway, and followed him out the door, down the maze of hallways back to the entrance they'd come in and to the parking lot.

"I hope it went better than it seemed like it was going to." She tried to make sure she kept her tone even. *Professional.* She'd heard Micah's boss use that word more than one time as his voice had boomed down the hallway, chasing after them like her past always had a way of doing to her.

"It did, believe it or not."

"I'm sorry my presence hurt things for you."

"It wasn't that… It was…" He trailed off, but Kate got it. It was a lot of things. Kate believed with all her heart that he was the best officer to have on this case. The amount he'd cared about his partner, the fact that he knew her and wanted to resolve the threat against her, those things were helping him, not harming his ability to handle the case objectively.

Right?

"So, back to Moose Haven?"

"Unless there's anywhere else you wanted to go." Kate was already shaking her head before she could get the sentence out. The sooner she could go back to the place she knew she belonged, the better. Much as she wanted to be with Micah, had relished the chance to be alone with him, her feelings were something she had to control. She cared about him too much to not consider the consequences of getting too closely involved at this point. He could be pulled from the case and she knew how much solving it meant to him.

"Sounds good."

The trip back to town happened without incident. Kate pretended to sleep most of the way, not wanting Micah to feel obligated to carrying on an awkward conversation with her. They were just outside Moose Haven when Micah's phone rang.

He answered and she listened. It was clearly someone on the police force, based on his questions, and anticipation built within her as she waited. The case could break today. And she was ready, more than ready, to have her life back.

What there was of it.

Micah hung up.

"Find out anything useful?"

"Yes, actually, a few things."

Kate waited, bracing herself for the weight she felt in his tone.

"We got ballistics back on the bullets that killed my partner." His voice was thick with feeling and she waited again while he took a deep breath.

"And?"

"The gun we found in the clearing is a match, as close as we can tell."

"So why did they leave it in such an obvious location?" She mumbled it more to herself than to Micah, but he shook his head anyway.

"It doesn't make sense. In good news, that's not all we learned."

"What else?" She felt herself leaning forward in her seat as she looked at him.

"Gabriel Hernandez had high levels of Rohypnol in his system."

"Wait, what? The date-rape drug?"

"Exactly."

The dots didn't take long to connect. "So someone drugged him, took him into the backcountry and set him up for an avalanche?"

"Give or take some details. That part is speculation." He studied her. "Unless I can get an avalanche expert to assess the scene and testify that something about it could only have been caused by a human-triggered avalanche."

"I don't know if that kind of evidence would still exist, if it ever did. Snow is tricky. And you still won't be able to prove motive. Someone could have triggered it accidentally."

"At the same time that Hernandez had a drug in his system that makes no sense unless our theory is correct?" Micah shook his head. "We'll need more evidence, but it's a start. It's enough to allow us to arrest a suspect for murder."

"Turn right. Then drive a quarter mile and turn left. It's a trail, but it's well used and you can probably make it up with your truck fairly close to the site," Kate said as they came up on West

Ridge Road. Micah did so, catching the tires on gravel, his turn was so fast.

"Site? Where are we going?"

"The scene of Hernandez's death, like you asked me to."

"I wasn't asking."

"Really? 'An avalanche expert'?"

"I can't ask that of you, Kate. It's avalanche territory, which is a level of danger I can't put you in. *Again.* I'll get someone else."

If only she knew whether he was truly concerned about that or if he just didn't want her involved for the sake of his job. She hadn't considered that. Micah was good at what he did, passionate. "I'm sorry—I forgot about your boss not wanting me involved." Kate blinked. Her stupid eyes were watering. Was there such a thing as winter allergies? Because it certainly shouldn't matter to her that she couldn't help him anymore. Not at all.

Except it did matter. Everything mattered when it came to Micah.

"It's not that, Kate."

"I was there—I heard him. Listen, seriously, you don't have to explain it to me."

Micah pulled the car over, shoved it in Park. "It's not that."

"Really? You're sticking with that story?"

"Would you quit arguing with me? You don't know what I'm thinking."

"I can guess?"

"Can you?" His eyes didn't leave hers. Not as he held her gaze, gave her reason to believe he meant what he said. Not as he moved toward her, angled his face down and met her lips in the slowest, most perfect kiss Kate had ever experienced.

It made her feel like she was eighteen again, free to fall in love without worrying about getting hurt, made her feel like they were the only two people on earth.

Like this mattered. Like it could last.

When he pulled back—too soon—she blinked. "Okay," she confessed, slightly breathless, "I admit it. I don't know what you're thinking."

"Or feeling." His voice was deep, husky and Kate swallowed hard, anticipating he'd move in for another kiss, but he didn't, just sat there and stared at her.

"Micah, we can't... You don't..."

"Don't tell me what I do or don't want." Had his voice lowered? Kate had never understood when Summer had turned into a mush pot around her now-husband Clay. Emma, sure, because she was a sweet woman and she was perfect for steady Tyler. Suddenly Kate understood. Here, in the front seat of the truck surrounded by spruce trees and snow, she knew.

She was in love with Micah Reed.

"But…think logically," she said aloud, not sure if she was talking to him or herself.

He leaned in a little and she jerked back, not ready to admit to him what she'd only just real- ized was true: that she loved him. Not ready to kiss him again. A first kiss, she could explain away. A second? She just couldn't. Love meant hurt. Ignoring her feelings was her only hope to protect herself. "Micah. The case."

It was like he flipped a switch. He turned for- ward, blinked his eyes. Cleared his throat.

"I'm sorry about the kiss. It won't happen again."

And then he drove.

Kate getting hurt was the last thing Micah wanted to let happen, which was why he'd been resistant to the idea of her taking him to the site of Gabriel Hernandez's recovery. And then he'd gone and kissed her, crossed a line he couldn't go back on.

And he'd hurt her. He'd seen it in her eyes when she pulled back when he'd been thinking of re- peating the kiss.

God, I am messing this up. The case, this sec- ond chance with Kate, all of it. Help me know what she needs.

He considered himself fairly good at understanding women as a general rule. But Kate took every single rule in the playbook, ripped it to shreds and then rewrote it in Russian or some equally confusing language. Nothing she did was what he expected, ever.

It was one of the things he liked about her.

It was one of the things that drove him crazy about her.

"Turn left onto this trail. You have four-wheel drive, right?"

Micah nodded, shifted into four-wheel and headed up the snowy trail, glad the car had enough clearance to make it over the bumpy snow. Barely.

"Stop here."

He did. And assessed the slopes above them. Perfect forty-five-degree angles, heavy with wet winter snow. Another slab could break free right now, take him and Kate with it.

Please, God, no.

It was all he could think to pray.

"Are you sure you want to do this?" he turned to Kate and asked, pushing through the tangle of emotions he felt every time he saw her, reminding himself that she was a capable woman and had the right to make her own decisions.

Wasn't that part of the reason he hadn't wanted Noah to take the lead on her protection? Because she didn't deserve to be trapped while they figured this out, just needed to be kept safe? And now he was doing the same thing.

"I'm sure."

Then he needed to let her be. "All right, show me." He zipped up his jacket, stepped out of the car and followed Kate to an impression about ten feet off the trail they'd driven on.

"We found him here."

Micah pulled a notepad out of his pocket, drew the basic gist of the scene and marked that location. He was no artist, but he could do enough to convey place.

It must not have snowed much on these mountains since the avalanche had happened, because Micah could still see it all clearly, the pile of snow, the way it had cut a path across the mountain.

"We didn't send a helicopter up. It's not protocol. But if you were really curious I'd say ask the troopers to bring theirs in and go over one of those two mountains." She motioned toward two he recognized from his childhood here as Desperation and Determination, twin peaks that stood above them. "Maybe there's evidence on one of the other faces?"

"It still won't be conclusive, though."

"Hence their brilliance in using an avalanche. They can be remotely triggered by movement or noise, and they wouldn't leave enough evidence of that to prove anything without a doubt. If that's what they used to do their dirty work."

Micah looked up at her, felt his eyes widen as her words triggered something in his mind. "Their dirty work…"

"Yes?"

"Let's go. Back to the car. We need to go to the police department."

Back in the car, he cranked the heat up and thought about what she'd said. "Dirty work" had somehow triggered the thought of cleaning up…

"And that's what they're doing with their entire operation."

"What, who is doing what?" Kate's response made him realize he'd spoken out aloud, even though he hadn't meant to.

"That's why we weren't able to identify who was in charge. He has been keeping himself out of the picture intentionally. Not only does he not plan to get caught, he doesn't even want to do this forever."

"The thefts?" Kate asked.

Micah nodded, grateful she was keeping up. He dialed Noah on his phone. "Noah, can you meet us at the police department? Thanks."

They pulled in ten minutes later and Micah walked Kate into the building as quickly as possible, remembering the last time they'd been there together. This time went off without incident, and soon they were in Noah's office, along with Erynn, who had been in there already and said she wanted to stay to learn what they knew.

Noah stood when they entered, then looked at Micah. "What did you learn in Anchorage?"

"First, think about this. What if the guy in charge is ready to close down the entire operation? I thought about this on the way back, starting with realizing that the thefts have stopped, had a month or so ago, much longer than their usual pattern. We weren't onto them when they stopped, so that wouldn't have been a reason. So what if that's why they quit stealing? Someone wanted to shut it down, get out before they got caught."

Noah nodded. "Okay, maybe."

"But no one else wants to." Micah was still working out the details, but sometimes talking through speculation helped, advanced a case.

"If he's in charge, it's probably not an issue. When he's gone, the contacts, whatever else he brings to the table, will all be gone too."

Micah continued, "Christopher Delaney's fingerprints were all over the gun we found in the clearing. It was left there, the gun that killed my partner."

Noah shook his head. "Ballistics were a match, then? I hadn't heard yet."

Micah nodded. "And someone left a murder

weapon in plain sight? Definitely not Christopher. That makes no sense. What if whoever is in charge left it there?"

"To implicate Christopher?" Kate asked.

Micah had almost forgotten she was there. But he nodded. "Exactly. And make me drop the case. I'd have gotten justice for my partner. If I were shortsighted enough that it was all I cared about, it would be easy to take that and end this now. But I'd still miss the one in charge."

"It's complete speculation," Noah reminded him. "You're reaching. I'm sorry—I know you want to solve this, but you're making connections that may or may not be there."

"Isn't that part of investigating?" Erynn chimed in. "Going with your gut and finding evidence to back it up?"

Noah winced. "It's a dangerous line to walk."

Micah agreed with Noah. "I think this is it. But I think I can find the rest if I take this trail." He didn't know why, but the way Kate had explained tracking, the way she needed to know details about the person she was tracking, made sense to him now more than ever. He felt like he was doing the same thing with this case, piecing together inconsequential details and making guesses. Noah was right that this bit was speculation. But it was the best educated guess he could put together. Nothing else explained the presence of the gun, as well.

"You have to go with your gut. See what you find," Erynn urged.

"You're sure?" Noah asked.

"I can't be sure." Micah realized the truth of the words as they left his lips. "But I do think this is the best way to go." The image of a trail came to him again. He was ready to track down the truth. "I'm going to find their cabin."

And hopefully find some justice for his fallen partner. And for Kate.

"So what do we do now?" Kate spoke up without thinking, but when three law enforcement agents swiveled toward her with eyebrows raised, she knew her mistake. She might have assisted in a variety of ways; Micah had been clear about that and thankful for it, but this was *their* case.

The past swirled into her present and haunted her with regret once again. What would it be like to work her own cases?

More and more, she'd wondered about it since all of this started. How was it that she could have lived her life here in Moose Haven for years, content with her daily penance for her inability to save Drew, the fact that she'd all but gotten him killed, and now she suddenly wanted more?

Was she selfish? Or was this part of that elusive "moving on" that everyone talked about? She didn't know.

But she did know, as sure as she was sitting here that not a single other person in this room was going to let her be involved.

Not even Micah. Something had changed in him, even more so since the kiss. Probably he'd finally listened to his boss, found that professional distance and realized that it was a bit more difficult to maintain with her following him around everywhere. Either that or he'd understood she had feelings for him and was putting her out of her misery the kindest way he could—by ignoring her embarrassing show of emotions.

Then again, he was the one who had kissed her. She'd kissed him back—oh, she'd *definitely* kissed him back—but he'd started it.

Kate didn't know what to think anymore. Except that she wasn't done with this case and had no intention of giving it up yet.

"Someone has to watch me, remember?" She batted her eyelashes and Noah laughed. Good, he was too serious these days, had been since a case had gone wrong a few years ago. Every now and then he was the lighthearted brother she remembered, but most of the time he ran on empty and acted like the weight of the world could crush him at any moment.

"You do need watching." Micah grinned at

her and the eyes swiveled to him. "But you can't come with me. I'm going deep into the mountains again. Like last time."

"Hopefully for your sake it won't be like last time." She tried to brush off his tone, the look on his face that left no doubts as to how serious he was. He didn't want her with him, wasn't even willing to talk about it, but that didn't mean she was done trying. "Please tell me no one in this room is going to lecture *me* about the dangers in the backcountry." They might have all the technical law enforcement skills and training, but Kate knew the woods and trails better than anyone, even Noah.

"It's too dangerous."

"We are not doing this again, having this same conversation." Kate shook her head. "I'm done with it. I'm an adult, I understand the risks and I want to help you find them. It's what I do, Micah. It's what I've trained my whole life to do." And it was.

"You're not coming, Kate. I'm sorry." And with that, Micah gave Noah a long glance, looked back at her one more time with something in his eyes she couldn't define and then walked away.

SIXTEEN

Micah was ready for the backcountry this time, ready for the group of men he was going to encounter. Not like last time. Micah's backpack was full of anything he could possibly use. He might not have Kate to help him find their trail, the location of Chris Delaney's cabin, but he had the things he'd learned from her. Hopefully that would be enough.

He wore his regular winter hiking boots but this time he had a pair of Kahtoolas around the bottom; the traction spikes just shy of crampon-level seriousness would ensure that he kept his footing, even if the trail turned icy. So far it was just soft snow with patches of dirt where it had melted away in the sun. Winter in this part of Alaska was variable at best—dumping feet of snow at once with little warning, or unseasonably warm temperatures that made the rest of the state jealous.

Micah had spent time before he left Moose

Haven looking at a topographical map, plotting out likely locations of the cabin. He'd heard rumors it was on Hope Mountain, but it seemed less likely now that he'd seen it again, and especially given the fact that Kate was extremely familiar with that area and wasn't aware of any cabins whose owners she didn't know.

That left Desperation and Determination as his most likely options, given their proximity to Hope Mountain, as well as the fact that someone had triggered an avalanche and would have had to have somewhere to go to avoid detection by the crews that would have swarmed the scene after Gabriel Hernandez was found.

Micah was fairly confident in Hernandez's guilt, though a dead man couldn't receive a fair trial and they'd never know for sure. His criminal record suggested he'd have experience with the kinds of jobs the Delaneys might have had him do.

The question of who had killed Jared Delaney was still grating at him. Not Christopher. So the guy in charge? Why would he kill his workforce? Unless he really was getting out of the business and needed to eliminate anyone who knew his identity. But if that was the case, why let Chris live?

He'd only get his answers straight from the source; he was fairly confident of that. Which was what drove him forward even as snow began to fall.

The trail he'd been following had been promising at first, enough of one to make him confident that he'd chosen the correct way to take. Now it had narrowed and he'd had to pick out his own path for at least a quarter mile a little farther back. He'd tried to pick a way that gave evidence of having been used lately, broken branches and the like, but he wasn't 100 percent sure he was going the right way.

The only consolation to the fact that he *might* be lost, and that if he wasn't lost he was walking into the most dangerous situation he'd faced yet, was that Kate wasn't here. He'd left her at the Moose Haven PD, with a cup of coffee and the look of someone who felt like she was being held captive.

Which, she sort of was, at least where Noah and Micah were concerned. But they were doing it benevolently. For her own good.

Micah followed the trail as it banked around the edges of the mountain, lost his footing but managed to catch himself on a branch. He took a breath, let it out slowly and took another step.

His foot came down sideways, not on the metal grips as it should have and he went down too, sideways, sliding six or so feet until he caught himself on a tree, by hitting it in the dead center of his kneecap.

Pain exploded in a dark rainbow and Micah swallowed hard. He'd felt soreness building in the knee the other day—one that had given him trouble during his high school basketball-playing days—but he'd taken some ibuprofen and told himself he didn't have time to let a doctor look at it and suggest anything stronger.

He took a breath, pulled himself back up toward the trail, only to have his knee give out again.

He'd rest for a few minutes. Five, maybe. Ten tops. That had to be enough to convince his knee to work with him.

Micah took a deep breath, let it out and looked around, feeling something was off.

Ahead of him and back up to the right, he caught movement in the trail. Just a branch, but something made him keep staring at it, take notice. Kate had made it clear that tracking wasn't all about what a person saw, but also what they felt.

Come on, God, help me see it. Whatever it is. His knee throbbed and Micah grabbed a handful of snow, held it against the snow pants he wore, hoping the cold would seep through some and help the swelling. Because he wasn't going to sit here any longer.

Not when he saw a figure move through the willow branches. Not Chris Delaney or another burly henchman of whoever's operation this was.

But Kate Dawson, head covered with a brown winter hat, dressed in dull colors, presumably to give herself the best chance of sneaking about undetected. His breath caught and for half a second he thought his heart might have quit beating. She was beautiful, stunningly so. And putting herself in very real danger that he couldn't allow her to face.

"Kate." He whispered it as loud as he dared, well aware of how sound carried in the cold winter air.

Either she didn't hear him or she was ignoring him. Hopefully the first, or he'd lecture her up and down when they got back to Moose Haven.

Assuming they made it back.

God, please.

Seemed like that was a lot of his prayers, lately, asking God for help.

His phone buzzed at his side. Amazing that he got service out here.

Noah's number.

Noah knew better than to call him when he was trying to sneak through the woods. Which meant if he was calling, there was a good reason.

"Hello?" He answered in a whisper, hoping he wasn't being tracked. And even if he was, fine. He was ready to face them, ready to end this. Micah took another glance in the direction where Kate was.

Make that *had been*. She was gone. Or invisible in the woods.

"We've got a problem."

"Tell me about it." Micah's hand rested on his injured knee. He'd told her to stay in town, made it very clear he could do this without her and needed to, and she'd still ignored him?

"Don Walters isn't dead."

A fist in the gut couldn't have caught Micah more off guard. "If he's not dead…"

"One small sample of blood matched Don's DNA, so he was there and was wounded. Someone had the smart idea to test more than one place, but those results just came in, since they weren't being rushed since we assumed we already had the answers we needed. The majority of the blood belonged to a man who was released in Anchorage several months back after some minor charges that weren't enough to hold him on."

"Another pawn in their group?"

"Guessing so."

"Which means Walters is now our chief suspect."

"In both the smuggling ring and several counts of murder."

Micah bit back any words that rose to the surface of his mind. *Sorry, God. Help me out here.* He squeezed his eyes shut, listened, but still heard no evidence of Kate's presence.

"It's worse than you think," Micah told Noah. "Your sister is out here."

"No way. She's in a room here at the station. Officer James is with her."

"Better go check. I just saw her in the woods and I have to go follow her." Into a more dangerous situation than any they'd seen before. They knew Don Walters's identity now, had evidence probably linking him to one murder and they would likely be able to find more.

This time, he had no reason not to kill them both.

"If she walks about with so much as a scratch…"

"Later, Noah. 'Bye." Micah hung up the phone. He didn't need Noah's threatening older-brother growl to give him sufficient motivation to find her.

She might be the only person in this life who'd ever cared enough about him to have his back even when he didn't want her to.

And he'd walked away from her, given himself excuse after excuse for why they shouldn't be together, hadn't even given her a choice. Just kissed her like he'd always wanted to, told himself the memory of it would have to be enough to get him through a lifetime alone.

But just like he should have given her an option to come with him today, make her own choices, and at least they'd have been in this mess *together*, he needed to give her a choice about this too.

And if Kate Dawson even had an inkling of inclination to give him a chance at a real relationship with her that went far beyond friendship, he had every intention of taking it.

Assuming they both got out of this alive.

Call it gut instinct—Erynn had when Kate had pleaded her case with the other woman and convinced her to let her out of police protective custody—but Kate felt like Micah was walking into a trap again. Which was why she'd decided to follow him. Not on the same trail he took, but keeping him in her general line of sight, crisscrossing his trail so he wouldn't get suspicious, but she wouldn't lose his position either.

He'd said that first day on the mountain, or the next, everything swirled together in her mind now, that he needed to figure out who was involved before he made any more steps. They still hadn't done that, and evidence had just continued to confuse everything.

As she crept through the narrowest game trail

she'd been able to pick out, one small enough she should be able to just blend in, even if someone looked directly at her unless they were an adept tracker, she thought through the case. What were they missing?

Someone had come after her. Then Don Walters had ended up dead, his body who knew where. Someone had shot at her in the woods, one of the Delaneys—Chris, she thought Micah had told her. Then Jared Delaney had tried to take a sniper shot at her and been killed by someone. Not his brother. Another man whose identity they were still missing. That man, presumably, left the handgun used to kill Micah's partner in a clearing. So that Micah would consider the case closed? So the man who'd killed his partner was dead and the rest of them could just…get away?

She moved behind a stand of spruce trees, stopped for a minute to catch her breath. She'd set a grueling pace, much faster than what they typically used during search-and-rescue missions, but she didn't want her trip to help Micah to turn into a recovery operation.

Couldn't even let her mind go there, not if she wanted to stay on top of her game and focused.

He'd gone off alone because of her, because he'd gotten too close. Not "professional" and couldn't stand to see her hurt.

But still, he didn't want her risking her life and she appreciated that.

And intended to ignore his preferences while she did that very thing. Because whether he realized it or not, Micah Reed needed her.

She'd snapped a picture of the map he'd been using at the police department, complete with marks indicating possible locations for Chris Delaney's cabin. She'd been thinking it through since then and he had some good guesses. She was heading to the one that seemed most promising.

Branches cracked somewhere to her left. Kate stilled. Listened with every sense she had.

There, down on the floor of the forest. Was that Micah? She leaned forward to see.

And felt rough hands on her shoulders yank her backward. She opened her mouth to scream only to have a hand clamped over her face.

Then something hit her on the head and dizziness swept over her. She wouldn't lose consciousness. Refused to…

The question bothering Micah most right now was Don Walters's mental state. Was he completely in control, and just pure evil? Or was the man crazy? He didn't know if one was better than the other for the sake of his and Kate's safety, wherever she was, and he didn't know which was true anyway.

Could be a little of both.

He looked around again. She'd disappeared without so much as a trace. And while he'd called her the backcountry ninja and meant it, he still felt uneasy. Just her being out here made Micah fear for her safety.

He kept walking, frowned a little. He should have reached the clearing by now, right? The one that would hopefully have the cabin? Micah glanced around the woods, looking for broken branches. Nothing around him. He backtracked until he'd reached the spot where he'd slid and got back onto the trail. Glanced over to where he'd seen Kate. Surely, even as careful as she was, she'd leave some unintentional evidence of where she'd gone. Maybe at this point tracking her was more important than continuing on the route he'd chosen.

There. He could see a broken bit of willow. He moved closer, frowned again.

An entire section of the brush was beaten down. Kate wouldn't have done that. He stepped carefully, making sure his feet didn't destroy any of the trail she or someone else had made in case he needed to analyze it again.

Someone less careful than Kate had been here. In an area, maybe two feet by two feet, someone had destroyed much more than she would have and Micah didn't have a good feeling about it at all.

Had someone taken her? Fought with her? He saw no signs of blood, no clothing torn on the branches. That was a good sign, at least.

He moved toward where he thought he could see a path. It was less than a game trail, but it was worth a try. The snow had frozen overnight and was mostly ice now, so any footprints from today weren't showing up, which was unfortunate. The new snow didn't amount to more than half an inch yet and he didn't see any signs of it being disturbed.

Micah debated his next move for about a minute before deciding that everything Kate had taught him meant that he should go with his instinct in tracking, go with what he knew not just about Kate, but about whomever was after her. They weren't going to take a trail; they were going to go the most difficult way possible. If he went to the right, he should end up fairly close to a cliff edge, at least he thought so from the time he'd spent looking at the map. It was as good a guess as any.

Please let me find her alone, God. Not in the clutches of a crazy man.

Micah moved through the woods, every sense on high alert in case someone was still out here, keeping watch. All of this was assuming he was right about their cabin being close by, but if he listened to his gut, he was pretty sure he was.

After at least half an hour of picking his way through thick tree limbs and over a couple of snow piles that had been disturbed recently— he thanked God for those and the confirmation they provided that he was on the right track—he could finally see it.

In a spot on the mountain where the trees cleared and were sparse, the cabin was exactly as he'd expected it to be. It was more practical than pretty, obviously built by the dwellers and not professionals, with a red tin roof that was faded in spots. He assessed it for weaknesses. The windows were high, but he might be able to climb into one undetected if it was the only option he had. The cabin was built on a platform; he might be able to go underneath. It would depend on where she was being held.

Assuming she was here.

He had to find her. She had to be here. Unless she was back in the woods somewhere, watching and hiding. He couldn't say for sure, so for now he had to act under the assumption that she'd been taken.

Micah moved toward the cabin, glanced down at his watch. Did he wait for darkness, when she could be in danger right now?

He couldn't.

But he had to. Going in too soon had been a mistake, had gotten Stephen killed, and while he knew his partner had agreed with the plan of action—it had even been his plan—that didn't mean Micah was going to be careless and repeat his mistakes.

"Come on, Kate. Stay safe. Hang in there."

And Micah crouched lower to the ground. Did the only thing he could do, which was wait.

And pray.

SEVENTEEN

The throbbing in her head was nothing compared to the wild percussion beat her heart was pounding out. Every fight-or-flight instinct seemed to have activated itself from the moment Kate had awakened from her not-so-pleasant nap.

She tried to sit up straighter in the chair where she was tied, but she just scraped her back on the rough wood and strained her hands against the ropes. They were bound well, with the skill of someone who knew what they were doing.

She turned her head, looked across the cabin to where Don Walters sat in front of the woodstove, drinking from a mug of what she assumed was coffee.

"I don't guess I could get some of that, could I?" She nodded her head to the mug. It didn't hurt to ask, and she was thirsty, not to mention desperately craving some of the clarity coffee occasionally provided.

Don shrugged. "I don't see why not." His voice

was calm. Not what she'd expected at all, nor was the way he walked over to the coffee maker and placidly poured her a mug. He stepped toward her, moving carefully so the liquid didn't spill, then stopped several feet in front of her. "You're smart enough to understand actions and consequences. If you try to use this as a weapon…"

She heard all he left unsaid, could use her imagination, though she'd really rather not. Kate just shook her head. "I won't."

He untied her hands, handed her the mug and she drank, watching him as she did so.

As she sipped the coffee—which was extremely full, dark and delicious—she made a mental list of what she knew. Wondered how many of the blanks she could get Don to fill in.

And wondered why he'd abducted her. And if he was already planning her death.

"More coffee?" He offered her a refill when she'd started to set the mug down and Kate nodded. She couldn't use the drink as a weapon, but drinking an excess of coffee would necessitate a trip to the outhouse, which could give her a chance to escape, find a way to defend herself, *something*.

And if none of her plans worked and today was her last day on earth, if she was meant to die, she may as well enjoy another cup of coffee before the end came.

"Why are you being so nice to me?" she asked after he'd sat.

"I've always been nice to you."

Kate raised her eyebrows. Sorted through the responses in her mind before deciding none of them were productive. If there was a chance she could talk her way out of this situation—something she doubted, but she was trying to stay positive—she needed to take it. Antagonizing him with sarcasm wasn't the right way to go. Not right now.

But trying to get more answers out of him? Not necessarily a bad idea. If she went about it the right way.

"Yes. You're right."

"Then again, I haven't ever abducted you before—is that what you're thinking?"

More or less. Kate shrugged, did her best to keep her face impassive.

"I have my reasons. No one said I was planning to hurt you."

She rolled her eyes. "You're not going to feed me some lines about how you'll let me live, are you? Because really I'm still feeling a little bad from the hit on the head and can't stomach it at the moment."

"Of course not. That's ridiculous. All I meant was that I wasn't going to hurt you."

Kate waited.

"I hire people for that sort of thing."

"Not all the time. I know of at least two men you killed yourself. Maybe three. I'm still deciding about Gabriel Hernandez, if that was you or your hired people."

He looked surprised, and not the kind someone could fake. She'd genuinely caught him off guard.

"I guess you're more intelligent than I gave you credit for. I never should have gone with the avalanche plan."

"You never should have broken the law."

"Speaking of not having the stomach for things, let's just stop that right there, shall we?"

"Works for me." Kate shifted in her seat, took another sip of coffee. "I am curious. What did I have that you wanted? Why ransack my house and cabin?"

Don shook his head. "Wasn't me. One of those ridiculous Delaneys I hired got it into his head that I'd hidden something in that jacket I repaired for you. I was only ever concerned about you being a threat because of what you'd seen."

"The avalanche that killed Hernandez?"

Don nodded, then shrugged. "The point is, I wasn't searching for anything. I only needed to scare you into silence. I figured finding a dead man in your house with some kind of warning would do that."

"So you killed the man whose blood we found with yours."

"Yes, and then faked my own death. I'd cut myself in the fight and realized if I left my car there, abandoned the store and then made it a target… it would look ideal, wouldn't it?"

To think she'd wasted even a second of sorrow on this man when she thought he'd been a victim. He was evil and manipulative.

Kate took a breath, tried to level her voice.

"Since we're shooting straight and you're going to kill me—excuse me, *have me killed*—anyway, mind filling in a few more details I hadn't quite figured out?"

"I do mind, actually." Don glanced at his watch.

"That's a bit petty, isn't it?" The words escaped before she could censor them, but clearly being polite wasn't winning her any favors anyway.

"I've been at this too long and seen too many people get cocky. You get cocky, you get caught. I've learned my lesson from their mistakes."

"You're already caught."

"By someone who will be dead in…" He glanced at his watch again. "Just a few hours."

"You're waiting till dark?" Kate did roll her eyes that time, didn't bother to hold back. "How classic."

"You know, on second thought, I will answer

a couple questions. If for no other reason than to prove to you I'm not the criminal you think I am."

"You're denying being a criminal?" Kate widened her eyes but he was already shaking his head.

"No. I don't deny that. But it's not what you think."

"I think you were in charge of the smuggling operation that Chris and Jared Delaney were running."

He looked bored. "That's not a question. I said you could ask questions, not bore me with your statements."

"Okay, fine. Did you kill Jared Delaney?"

"I did."

"Why?"

"He wouldn't listen anymore. His brother was easier to mold, to convince of things, but Jared didn't follow directions well. I told him we had to end the smuggling ring, get out of town and possibly the country while we'd still escape detection, and he wouldn't agree. Kept trying to make deals without me." Don shook his head again. "He had to go."

"Why do it? You had a legitimate business, a place in town."

He walked away from her, paced back in her direction. "Ever hear of being in the wrong place at the wrong time?"

"I'm familiar with the phrase."

"It's how I met the Delaneys. They had started the smuggling ring, but were sloppy. I could tell they were going to get caught. I knew how to run a legitate business, as you put it, I knew my skills could be put to good use, finding targets and facilitating their…acquisition, and I needed the money. Business hasn't been good. I could have lost my house." He shrugged.

"That's it? You threw everything away for that?"

"Enough talking. Sit still and shut up." He took the coffee and bound her hands again. Then he walked away from her, sounding nothing like the man whose store she'd grown up going to. So he would react when agitated even if he was fairly good at keeping his cool most of the time. It was good information to know, could be useful to her later, when she figured a way out of this.

Kate used the break in conversation to assess the cabin itself. Even her cabin had homier touches—thanks to Summer, who had hiked out with her once and declared it not "cozy" enough. This place had none of that. The walls weren't Sheetrocked, just made of plywood. That was good to know. Breaking through a wall was a possibility. Her eyes moved to the windows. Another option for her escape, though she expected if she was left alone the windows would probably be secured somehow. Or Don would count on the likely futility of escape to try to deter her from trying anything.

If her life were a movie, this would be the part where the hero burst in to save her. But Kate wasn't that kind of heroine anyway. *She* did the saving. For a living, in fact. How ironic if she really did die here, if she couldn't save herself.

Of course, her life was full of irony already, saving people from avalanches every winter when she hadn't been able to rescue one of the people who had mattered most in her life.

Micah was up here somewhere, that much she was sure of, trying to track down the cabin where she was, since presumably it belonged to the Delaneys.

She'd seen no sign of any other people since she'd awakened. Was the remaining Delaney brother—what had his name been… Christopher?—outside keeping watch? Or had Don gotten rid of him like he'd killed Jared Delaney?

Kate's headache worsened and she wished she had a hand free to rub it. A plan…she needed a plan.

She leaned back and closed her eyes against the daylight. Another hour and it would be dark. Not something that boded well for her well-being, but at least maybe her headache would improve. For a moment as she rested her eyes, she let herself dream about being that kind of woman—the kind who needed a man to rescue her. Or at least appreciated it when he did. Micah would sweep in here, disarm Don of the .44 bear gun he had at his hip and sweep Kate away to safety. Maybe ride off into the sunset after that.

But again, she was Kate Dawson. Capable. Not in need of saving.

Except by God. Would He still save her if she asked?

Her throat tightened and she swallowed hard. Now wasn't the time to get caught up in regrets, think about the faith she'd mostly walked away from.

Nor was it the time for daydreams about Micah. He had a case to work on. She'd helped him with it and now she was in the way. Isn't that why she'd been left behind? So she wouldn't become a liability?

Too bad she'd become one anyway.

But Micah knew his job, knew if it came down to it he needed to focus on arresting the people behind all this.

Not saving Kate. No, that part was up to her.

If he had to sit here for one more minute, Micah was going to lose his mind.

He'd heard voices, too dim to make out the words, for a few minutes a while back. One of them was female and he was almost positive it was Kate. So she was alive. In what condition, he couldn't be sure, but there was still hope.

The weak winter sun had finally faded from the sky and Micah was ready to act. He'd moved toward the cabin until he was underneath as soon as it had become dark enough that he'd been fairly certain no lookouts could see him. So far he'd only seen Christopher Delaney. No signs of any other people. Which meant the people in the cabin might just be Don and Kate.

The thought of her facing a murderer alone was enough to make him sick, but he tried to focus instead on the fact that it was one against one in there and Kate wasn't the kind to give up. If anyone had a chance, it was her.

The image of Jared Delaney, dead on a cliff side, rose in his mind, followed quickly by several other bodies for whom Don was responsible and Micah had to remind himself to breathe.

Keep her safe, God. Rescue her. Through her, me, whoever, but rescue her.

He crept beneath the cabin's foundation, finding it was constructed much the way he'd assume it would be, but taking note of possible weak spots in the floor—he'd found one that looked promising—and anything else that could possibly help him.

A door creaked open.

Micah sat still, somewhere toward the middle of the cabin and squinted out into the darkening blue of the winter night. The noise had come from the front door, closer to the cliff, and he focused his attention that way. Something else creaked. The stairs?

Then he saw one set of legs. Two. Walters and Kate. She was in front of him. They were leaving the cabin after sunset… It didn't bode well for what Walters had planned for Kate. Micah took one last look above him, wondering what kind of evidence was inside. Everything he needed for his case against Christopher Delaney and Don Walters was here, close enough to touch.

But Kate was leaving the cabin. And given a choice between following her to try to make sure she got out of this alive, and getting his evidence…

Kate was what really mattered. Micah shook his head, almost surprised at himself for letting his thoughts for her intrude again when he'd think he would be focused on the danger in front of them. This case had gotten personal, maybe more than he'd anticipated. But he could think about that more later. Right now was the time for action.

He pulled his phone out of his pocket, and texted his boss the GPS coordinates along with a message. After all this, after pushing Kate away so he could see the case through, he was handing it over, at least in part, to someone else.

Because he wasn't his parents. And while he believed in his work, was proud of what he did and would work hard at it with everything, he wasn't his parents.

People were more important. And Micah knew it.

He turned his attention back to the front steps, and the noise that sounded like someone stumbling. Kate?

"I said hurry up." He heard the man—Walters—bite the words out, his voice rough.

"If you'd untie me, I could walk a lot faster."

She tripped as she said it, fell to the ground, and it took everything in Micah not to crawl toward her, bring her underneath the cabin's foundation with him. But it would be a false sense of security and would last for seconds. They'd still be killed, just together.

But he did stare at her, let his eyes meet hers. Kate's green eyes widened. She saw him. Micah couldn't begin to sort through the emotions he felt, tightening his chest, making it harder to breathe. Fear for her safety tangled all together with something he didn't think he'd felt before, at least not like this.

He loved her.

He couldn't give her the kind of life her parents

had. But he'd been making her decisions for her for too long now. He loved her. And it was time to let her choose whether or not she wanted to do anything about that.

But first he had to get them both out alive.

Kate stood back up and he felt the loss of her eye contact like something had been ripped away from him. He wanted her back. Safe. Now.

Micah took a breath. *You've taken care of her for this long, God, when I hadn't realized how much I cared about her. Please don't let me lose her now.*

"Let's go." Walters's voice had grown even colder and Micah could see that Kate's stumbling was genuine. At least mostly. She might be playing it up a tad to get Walters to untie her, but in addition to the rope binding her hands behind her back, which he'd noticed when she'd fallen earlier, her legs were bound loosely at her ankles.

Navigating the mountain safely like that was going to be nearly impossible. If Walters didn't kill her, falling down the mountain might.

"Fine. Be still."

Walters bent, untied her ankles, but didn't lower his head enough to look under the cabin. Micah took a deep breath, let it out slowly. As long as he didn't do anything stupid, he wouldn't be seen or caught under here. But how he was going to avoid detection while they went wherever they were going was a different story.

But he was following them. That much he'd made up his mind about.

He waited until they'd left the clearing and entered the woods before he made his move, creeping to the edge of the cabin. He'd just been about to step into the open when Christopher Delaney appeared, followed Walters and Kate. Was Delaney still working for Walters? If their theory was correct, Walters had killed Jared. Christopher couldn't have just accepted that. Having a possibility that the criminals might turn on each other was a good thing, that Micah hoped would come to fruition.

When Delaney was into the woods a bit, Micah followed, making quick work of the open area to get back into the low willow branches. Enough new snow had fallen in the last couple hours that their footprints were easy to see; no need to use his new tracking skills, and he was thankful for it. There was too much on his mind.

Don Walters had fooled them all for years, not shown his true colors. Micah had known him since he was a kid. Did his criminal ways go back that far? It would be interesting to find out and he looked forward to having some answers. Right now it just stung that he hadn't seen who was behind it all until it was too late and the man had Kate.

Still, wishing that fact away wouldn't do any good. All he could do now was follow them.

So he did, around willows, through the branches and farther up the mountain toward the openness of the tree line. They were making good time and the space between Delaney and Walters and Kate had closed while Micah had fallen back behind them some. Micah picked up his pace, his knee throbbing in pain, even as he shook his head at the terrain they were heading through. Snow was still falling and the wind was blowing enough to make the snow fly around, almost blinding him. Ideal for avalanche conditions, Kate had to have already noticed.

Help her not be afraid, God. Her fear of avalanches was earned, well understandable. But whether or not one was avoidable tonight was questionable at best.

The entire night was ripe for disaster.

Micah kept his eyes on Kate, hurried his footsteps and kept praying that he wasn't too late. Not too late to tell Kate he loved her, not too late to bring justice, not too late to get them all down the mountain safely.

EIGHTEEN

The biting wind tore at Kate, but she'd worn her best gear on this now-failed mission, the one thing she'd done right, and the only part of her that was cold was her ears.

And the pit in her stomach that grew both colder and heavier with every step they took up the mountain. They'd been following a trail that had seen some use until a little while ago, when they'd started breaking new ground. Kate was light enough that she'd managed to stay on top of the frozen snow most of the time, but every now and then she'd break through and post hole, her foot breaking through the first layer of snow and plunging her into snow deeper than her leg.

It was overwhelming, considering the amount of snow built up around them, below them and most especially above them. The snow fell thick and heavy, adding a slab of snow to the already unstable pack around them, and they were trekking up the mountain like they were immune to the forces of nature.

She felt her breathing grow shallower as she surveyed the perfectly angled slopes, felt her mind start to flash back to *that day*, to *her* avalanche. Hers and Drew's. It hadn't been on this mountain. But the day had been similar, a bad day to be in the backcountry, and she'd pushed them in anyway.

This time she didn't have a choice. She glanced over at Walters, in front of her and slightly to the left. Looked at the Delaney brother who was behind them. He'd stayed back a bit, presumably just in case someone got the crazy idea to come rescue her. She didn't think Walters had noticed him. Interesting.

And speaking of crazy rescue ideas, Micah had plenty in his mind; she'd seen it in his eyes when their gazes had locked on each other at the cabin. It gave a small part of her heart hope to know that while she'd been in the cabin wishing he'd come rescue her, he had been there, had been working on doing just that.

And then they'd left. And they needed a new plan B again.

Kate glanced at the slopes. Reminded herself that they weren't sentient or vengeful. They didn't force avalanches to come down on unsuspecting high schoolers. They didn't steal lives. They were part of nature, the world God had created.

Did that mean God had caused the avalanche? Kate didn't know and realized now that maybe she never would, but it was time to stop acting like He had it out for her. She'd believed in Him for her entire life, had let her faith guide her choices for many years, from the time she was small. By the time she'd lost her parents, Kate had already mostly walked away from her Heavenly Father.

It hurt too much to wonder if He was there to comfort her during loss, or if He was the one who caused it. Sovereignty was a lovely concept until you had to apply it to your life, and there, Kate found, was the rub.

How strange, she thought in a slightly detached way, that in what could be her last moments on earth, she was spending them thinking about her shattered relationship with God, wondering if it was too late to fix it.

She glanced up at the mountain again. They were leading her somewhere, and she knew it wasn't anywhere good. Given how people who had opposed Walters had ended up dead, Kate suspected they were taking her somewhere to kill her.

Did she keep following them, try to find a safe

way to save herself? Or was the very slope she feared the best hope she had of saving herself?

Kate swallowed hard, remembering the words from earlier. Maybe the better question was, was it the best hope she had of God saving her?

Nothing was safe about that slope, the conditions, the backcountry as a whole. But maybe safety wasn't the answer.

God, I'm sorry for walking away from You. I know more than most that You're not safe. But you are good.

Please save me.

Kate looked up the mountainside. Took a breath, and started to run.

Up.

Micah saw the moment Kate split from her group and started to sprint up the mountain and he almost forgot to breathe. She was headed up, straight into avalanche territory, flirting with danger in a way he'd have been sure she'd never do.

But he saw the method to it, knew she'd done the unthinkable, not because she wanted to die but because she wanted to live. It was a bold move, even for Kate, but he admired it, even while it scared him to death.

No sense in keeping his position secret now. He ran ahead, turned toward the upper slopes and hoped he'd be able to catch her, but he was heavier and couldn't run on top of the packed snow like she could. His legs sank and no matter how much energy he used, his pace was a slow walk at best.

They'd seen him now; he could tell by the commotion over in the direction where the men were. Not far enough from Kate for comfort.

She'd heard them too and he saw her glance backward, change her course slightly. She was heading back down, cutting in front of the men who were after her. She must be hoping to get under them again, then double back onto their packed trail. Micah liked the decision. She was smart to stay off the top of the mountain when she could, and she'd only gone up there out of necessity. She wasn't flirting with danger. She was making smart choices.

He smiled for half a second, before the full gravity of their situation hit him all over again. He glanced at the slope.

They had to get out of here.

A gunshot echoed through the air and Micah heard the bullet as it passed, then yelling from Delaney and Walters as the snow rumbled beneath them. Another shot, this one toward Kate. It missed her, because she kept running.

He looked up at Kate, feeling the distance between them and knowing the two hundred yards might as well be two hundred miles for all the help he'd be to her. Desperation crushed his lungs, stole his breath, and he wanted to scream but knew that if the shots and yelling hadn't set off an avalanche yet, his voice could be the thing to send it over the edge.

God, help her.

He prayed as he heard a crack, dove to the ground as his mind registered the sound first as a gunshot and then realized it was the snow breaking loose, a slab of it one hundred yards above Kate and slightly to the left. She'd be on the edge of it, maybe.

Run, Kate, run. He stared at her, willing her to pick up the pace, as he stood up, out of the path of the devastating slide, knowing he couldn't do anything to help her. He'd known theoretically that she was in God's hands and no matter how much he wanted to sweep in and be the one who rescued her, he also had to learn to be still. Let God save her.

Please, God. Please.

There was snow everywhere, heavy, pressing against Kate, making it hard to breathe. She'd never thought she'd be here again, caught in a raging river of snow that didn't care if she lived or died. Alone in the endless white.

God is good. God is good. Repeating it helped

it sink into her heart, gave her a rhythm to sync her breath to, reminded her to breathe when gut instinct told her to stop, lest the snow get in her mouth. But she had to keep breathing, had to override her body's protective instincts, if she wanted to live.

Her arm caught on something. Ice? A rock? Kate didn't know but it hurt and she fought the urge to pull it toward her to protect her, kept using it to "swim" in the snow, her arms moving like a freestyle swimmer, like she'd learned in the many survival skills training sessions she'd been part of.

The slide had broken loose after the gunshot and yelling, and Kate had been back in her past again, standing with Drew and staring as the mountain started chasing them. She could hear his screams, hers, even though she was silent this time.

She'd prayed, that time and this time. She was finally able to understand that even if she died in this avalanche, even though Drew had died in the last one she'd been caught by, God was still good.

Now and always.

But please, God, if it's okay, I'd really rather live. I want to tell Micah I love him.

Kate kept trying to work with the snow, not against it, tried to stay on top of the seemingly endless white wave, but snow pounded her, fought her.

Please, God.

And then the snow had her, swallowed her in its inescapable grip. And the white all turned to dark. And went still.

She carved a space for herself with her hands, making as much room in her little cave to breathe as she could. Prayed her avalanche beacon worked.

And waited for rescue, knowing that at least she wasn't alone. God had never left her before. Wouldn't leave her now.

No matter what happened.

The river of snow continued down the mountain, washed over Kate in waves. Micah kept his eyes on the spot where she'd been until he saw the dark of her winter gear being pulled in the current of snow. At least she was near the top; he knew where she was. He followed her trail down the mountain, and the snow finally hit a ravine, down below where Micah was, and stopped.

No sign of Kate. Micah swallowed hard, his mouth dry, heart pounding. Surely he wouldn't come this close to finding the courage to tell her how he felt, only to lose her.

God, help.

Micah backtracked on the trail, toward where

Kate was, running as fast as he could, his mind counting seconds almost unconsciously. The survival rule of threes kept repeating in his mind, to the cadence of his steps as he ran. Three weeks without food, three days without water, three minutes without air.

Three minutes. If the snow had packed firm enough around her like it often did, then Kate had three minutes.

And Micah had three minutes to find her.

"Kate!"

He glanced around as he ran, looking for the men who'd been behind all this but seeing nothing. Either they'd used the avalanche and gotten away, or more likely they'd been swept away in the same avalanche as Kate.

He didn't want them to die like this, didn't want them to walk without paying the legal consequences for their crimes. And Micah had questions he wanted answered.

But Kate was his first priority.

He hit the emergency transmit button on his satphone and prayed help would find them, but knew by the time anyone else arrived, their focus would only be on recovering the bodies of avalanche victims. Any rescues would have to take place right now, this moment.

He moved to the last place he'd seen Kate, swung his backpack around to the front and pulled the small shovel off it, as well as the avalanche beacon he had in his pack. Had Kate been wearing one? He hadn't seen for sure, but surely when she'd set off to find the cabin she'd been prepared. He hoped.

The beacon beeped, not close enough together to tell him he was anywhere close. He tracked over the snow, counting seconds.

Fifty-eight. Fifty-nine. Sixty.

Two minutes. He had two minutes left.

The beeping of the beacon had started to sound, alerting him to the presense of another beacon—Kate's—nearby, but not speeding up like it would if he was close. The noise was mocking him and Micah wanted to yell, kick the snow and pitch a fit like he'd seen a kid in the grocery store doing last week in Anchorage, but he was an adult, a law enforcement officer, and he had to keep his cool, try something different.

Right or left?

He moved to the right, going more on instinct than anything else. The beacon beeped in the background. Maybe with more frequency? He stopped to listen. He wasn't imagining it; it was picking up on something. He moved slightly left.

The beeps got closer together, until the beacon was nearly frantic enough to keep up with the beating of Micah's heart. He threw himself to his knees, small shovel in hand, which he'd had in his backpack in case of avalanche danger, and started to dig, using the probe he'd also had attached to his backpack to guide him. The long stick was essential in avalanche rescues, providing a way to poke through the thick snow to find a person beneath it.

Micah hit something with the probe, about two feet below him. Micah poked again, gently.

Someone grabbed it, pulled it deeper into the snow, and his eyes widened as he doubled his speed with the shovel.

Ninety-six. Ninety-seven. Ninety-eight.

They were running out of seconds.

Something black came into view, buried in the snow, and Micah frantically brushed the snow away, shoved the heavy piles farther back.

It was Kate.

But was she moving? Breathing? She'd grabbed the pole but even that had been twenty seconds ago. A lot could happen in that time.

"Kate!"

Movement. She was moving. Micah pushed his hands through the snow, wrapped them around her, best he could, and pulled her toward him.

The snow released its grip on her. And she was free.

He fell backward, and she came with him, tumbling for a brief moment into his lap and then beside him.

Thank You, God.

He rolled over, sat up and looked at her.

She smiled. "You came."

"I did. So did you."

"I couldn't let you do it alone."

"Me neither." Micah swallowed hard. "But, Kate, we were never alone. You know that, don't you?"

"I do." She brushed something from her cheek. A tear? Snow? He didn't know. But it didn't seem to matter because her eyes shone with a light he hadn't noticed in them the last time they'd talked, the one he'd seen there when they were kids.

Faith.

"Where are the men? Don? Christopher?" Kate asked and Micah looked around again. Shook his head. "If they were caught in that…" He didn't finish, but Kate knew the rest. It had been more than three minutes.

"We have to try." She stood, brushing snow from her pants, and Micah did the same, taking his shovel and his probe. They dug up the surrounding area, worked together to try to find the men who'd attempted to kill her, until a chopper finally arrived.

Micah turned to Kate as the chopper landed, shouting above its noise, "We tried, Kate. But it's over." He wished they'd been able to stand trial for their crimes, but justice had been served, even if not the way he'd have preferred or expected. But it was over. And it would have to be enough for him.

"It is." She nodded, took a breath and sighed. "I'm tired."

"Let's get you back home."

NINETEEN

Once Kate had been checked out by an EMT and was safely on her way to Moose Haven Lodge, and Micah knew the bodies of the two men had been recovered and this was really over, he walked into the conference room at the Moose Haven Police Department, where his boss was waiting.

"Evidence in the location you sent us to was gold, Reed. You and Officer Searls had been close, when you came down to arrest the Delaneys. Everything there backs up what we had."

"And includes Don Walters?"

Chief Clark nodded. "The one piece you had been missing."

The leader of the group. Some piece to miss. Micah still felt the loss of Stephen, would probably dream about that last shootout for a while. But he knew they'd done everything they could, had followed procedure and it just hadn't gone the way they'd have wanted.

At least they'd found the criminals responsible and ensured they were done killing people to hide their crimes. He'd rather they'd have gone to prison for years but in the end that choice hadn't been his. Their own decisions had led to their deaths, just like their decisions would have led to their time in prison.

"Officer Reed?" the chief started to say. Micah took a breath, braced himself. "I don't apologize. You know that. But I wanted to make sure you knew, you handled this case well. And the fact that you rescued the woman…"

Here it was, the reminder of how letting this get too personal could affect his police work.

"You were a hero today. People are what matter, Reed. The only reason we don't want cases to get personal is sometimes caring too much can actually hurt. In this case, it didn't. You did the right thing—you did good work." The chief nodded. "Very good work."

It was the highest praise the man offered, and Micah soaked it in. "Thank you, sir."

"You can fill out the incident paperwork in the morning. I'm leaving it here for you and I expect you back in Anchorage as soon as possible."

"I may need to take a couple of personal days."

The chief cracked half a smile. "That's fine. I hope it goes well for you."

Micah smiled back. "Thank you, sir."

And headed for the lodge and the woman he loved.

A long shower, a pair of pajamas she'd borrowed from her sister that were too long for her but blissfully cozy and one warm blanket later, Kate sat by the fire in one of the leather chairs in her family's private section of the lodge. She was finally almost warm.

"You're sure you're okay?" Noah asked for the fifth time in as many minutes.

"I'm still sure, Noah." And she was. For the first time in years, Kate felt like she could take a full, deep breath. The weight she'd carried was gone, the responsibility to save other people that she'd thought was hers... God was the one who saved, the one who gave and took away, and it was time she let Him do His job.

Not that being a rescuer was wrong. It was a noble calling and one she was thankful to have gotten to fill for so many years. But she was ready to try her hand at another kind of rescuing.

"You look like you're thinking something," Noah commented and Kate nodded.

"I am."

"Going to tell me what it is?"

"I think I have to talk to someone else first." Kate tried to stay vague, but offered her brother a smile. Overprotective as he was, he did love her, and she was thankful for that. She'd miss him when she left Moose Haven.

Because she was leaving. Had no real reason to stay and wanted to try giving some of her dreams a chance. First, though, she wanted to talk to Micah.

See if maybe…he wanted to fit into those dreams too.

Noah had come home to be with Kate while Micah wrapped up the case, had filled her in on the details. Don Walters had, indeed, been the one behind the crime ring, the one responsible for finding targets, orchestrating their theft and smuggling them to buyers in various locations. Chris Delaney's cabin in the mountains where she'd been held had given enough evidence to be able to convict him of that and several of the murders. However, both Don Walters and Christopher Delaney had died in the avalanche they'd caused, which left a bitter taste in Kate's mouth. She'd have rather they paid for their crimes in prison. It didn't seem fair, but as she was trying to remind herself, God was good and He worked things out the way He wanted.

"I'll miss you, you know." Noah spoke up and Kate met his gaze, eyebrows up.

"I'm losing my touch if I'm that easy to read."

He laughed. Really laughed, a sound she hadn't heard from him much in years. He'd gotten far too serious lately and Kate still wondered why, though she respected his privacy enough not to ask. "You're not that easy to read. You're still Kate. Just…maybe a little softer."

"Repeated near-death experiences will do that to a person." She quirked an eyebrow.

"Maybe you should try to lay off those for a while. Do something safe for a change."

Now it was Kate's turn to laugh. Safety had just never fit that well into her plans for life. "I'll see what I can do."

"I'm hoping to help out with that." Micah's voice in the doorway made her heart jump and Kate grinned, turned toward him.

"Hi. Long time no see."

"I had some things to wrap up." He walked toward her and she was sure his shoulders were broader than they had been. In any case, he held them higher and she could tell she hadn't been the only one changed by the ordeal. He was different too. And she couldn't wait to hear all about it.

Maybe spend the rest of her lifetime hearing about that and every other thing about him that fascinated her.

"I think this is my cue to leave." Noah smiled, shook his head. "You kids try not to get into any trouble. It's been a full week and I think we're all ready for a bit of a break."

Kate couldn't deny the relief that came from knowing no one was chasing her anymore, that she was free to live her life without looking over her shoulder. There had been so many variables, so many holes in the justice system, that she knew their deaths were the only thing that virtually assured she was free from the terror they'd caused. So while it saddened her, she was thankful for God's mercies to her, the way He took care of her, even in ways it was hard to wrap her mind around.

Noah walked out the door Micah had just come in and Micah took the leather chair next to Kate, reaching out for her hand. She kept one hand on her knit blanket around her and stuck the other through toward him, let him intertwine their fingers. The way their hands caught together was magic itself, and Kate knew, really knew, that this was the man she'd been waiting to meet. The only one who could make her consider settling down.

Though she hoped he had a pretty loose interpretation of "settling down," since she'd already called her acquaintance in Anchorage, given him a verbal commitment that she'd be filling out an online application for the next Trooper Academy. Where they took her after that…she didn't know.

"I missed you, Kate." Micah squeezed her

hand, smiled at her as he met her eyes, their faces only a foot apart.

Her eyes flickered to his lips and she swallowed, bit her bottom lip and met his eyes. "I missed you too, but it was only a couple hours, you know."

"A couple hours too many. And besides, I meant for the last several decades. I don't know if I ever said it but I missed you then."

"Oh."

"And I should have told you goodbye all those years ago. I thought..." Micah shrugged. "I didn't think it would matter to you. And it mattered too much for me to be able to do it."

His words made sense, tangled as the emotions behind them were. "It's okay—it's in the past."

"I know. But the past can impact the future and I want to make sure we're starting fresh."

"Starting what fresh?"

"This." He gestured between them. "This relationship that I'm hoping to start with you."

"Micah, I..."

"Wait, I have to say this first. I have to stop making your decisions for you, trying to keep you safe. I've spent years thinking I wasn't good enough for you, that I couldn't give you the kind of life you had growing up, only to realize—"

"I don't even want that kind of life now. I loved how I grew up, but it's not the way my life is now."

"Exactly. I realized I was making your choices for you."

Kate nodded. "I have to tell you before you say anything else, that I'm applying for the next Trooper Academy. I've got a friend at the troopers who's been hounding me for years…"

"Good. You should."

Kate blinked. She'd known he was special, but if that announcement didn't even make him flinch, then maybe she hadn't realized how special.

"It doesn't change anything about what I want to say."

Had she read him wrong, or…? Her heartbeat quickened.

"Kate Dawson, I should have told you years ago that I love you. Because I do, and it's only grown over the years. I love you, and I don't want to spend any more of my life without you. I don't have a ring because even though this isn't new, I wasn't planning on needing an engagement ring when I came down from Anchorage to make arrests. But I want to marry you and spend the rest of my life having adventures with you."

It was almost like he was asking…

"Kate, will you marry me?"

She met his eyes, felt her face curve into a smile. Laughed. "Yes, yes I will." And then moved in for a kiss.

EPILOGUE

Winter had turned to spring and Kate had finished the spring semester at the Alaska State Trooper Academy, graduated at the top of her class. And Micah had waited for her to finish.

Now it was summer and tonight, the wait for her to become his wife was over. She'd not cared much about the details of the wedding and had left many of them to her sister and sister-in-law to handle. Micah had worked with the two of them to get Kate's cabin in the woods fixed up, all evidence of destruction cleaned up, new windows put in. They were getting married in a mountain clearing nearby, having a reception at the ceremony site and then the guests would head back down the mountain and Micah and Kate would start their honeymoon in her cabin and begin their lives as a married couple where they'd been brought back together.

Micah looked at himself in the mirror, took a deep breath. He still couldn't believe he'd be a husband in less than an hour. Part of him still wanted to go make sure Kate didn't feel like she was making a mistake, settling for a man who didn't want a white picket fence but instead wanted to do the job he did, take the risks he was willing to take.

Then again, Kate wasn't much of a white-picket-fence girl. With one more glance at the mirror, he walked out of the cabin.

A flash of white disappeared around the corner outside, and a shriek surely too girly to be Kate came from the side of the house.

Still, though, who else would be in white today of all days? Kate had let her bridesmaids, Summer and Emma, choose their own dresses in navy blue. No, it had to be his bride.

"Kate?"

"Don't make another move, Micah Reed." Her voice was full of laughter, but as bossy as ever and he stopped moving. "It's bad luck to see the bride in her dress before the ceremony."

"Considering that we've survived being shot at, a trip wire, a sniper and an avalanche together, I'm willing to tempt fate and see you."

"Nope, this is the one tradition I care about. Go to the clearing and I'll be up there in just a few minutes."

Micah shook his head. Life with her wasn't going to be boring, not ever.

He took the track up to the site where the wedding would take place, taking a deep breath of the summer air. The sky was perfectly blue, a rarity for this part of the Kenai Peninsula, even in June.

Thanks, God, for even taking care of the weather.

They'd discussed the dangers of an outdoor wedding in Alaska, but Kate had just laughed, something she was doing a lot more of lately, and said she didn't care as long as they got married.

Sounded good to Micah.

The sunshine was still a nice surprise. He walked to the front of the clearing, smiling at the family and friends who had joined them. His parents were here, even, having taken time off work for the wedding. His dad had even said something to him that morning about how they were sorry they hadn't spent more time with him back then. Maybe it wasn't too late for their relationships to change too. Maybe every family didn't have to be exactly alike to be a good one. All Micah knew today was that he wanted a family with Kate Dawson. Wanted to watch her walk down the aisle toward him in just a few minutes and change her last name to Reed. Wanted a chance to make their own future. Together.

Micah stopped at the front, listened to the flute music that a friend of Kate's from the search-and-rescue team had agreed to provide. Theirs was a low-key wedding, but it was perfectly Kate, and that was what mattered to Micah. She'd be happy.

And he'd be happy having her as his wife.

The music changed and the guests, sensing the shift, turned back in their seats.

There was Kate, at the end of the clearing, smiling up at him. Her dress was simple, but more elaborate than he'd anticipated, lace draped around her shoulders, the neckline dipping to a front V. The fitted bodice led to a flowing train, which dragged behind her on the moss ever so slightly.

If he was dreaming this moment, he couldn't have dreamed it more perfectly. She was beautiful. Inside and out.

As she walked to the front, he didn't break eye contact with her. It was hard to believe they were here, really getting married, after all the years in their friendship, all they'd been through.

But it was true, it was happening and Micah couldn't be happier.

"Dearly beloved, friends and family of Micah and Kate, we are gathered here today…"

The Moose Haven Community Church pastor spoke but Micah didn't hear a word. All he could do was stare at Kate, tell God over and over how thankful he was for her.

They said their vows, made their promises. Micah meant every word and knew Kate did too;

a love like theirs, forged in fire as it was, would stand up to every test with God to help them. He had no doubts.

"You may kiss your bride."

And kiss her he did.

* * * * *

Go back and check out the first two Dawson family adventures in the beautiful Alaskan wilderness:

Mountain Refuge
Alaskan Hideout

Find these and other great reads at www.LoveInspired.com

Dear Reader,

Thanks for coming back to Moose Haven with me! I have had so much fun setting these books in a fictional town in Alaska's very real Kenai Peninsula, a place I love to go to get away. If you ever find yourself in Alaska and want to pretend you're in Moose Haven, feel free to visit Seward, Alaska, one of the best towns I've ever been to. It's much like the fictional town it inspired, tucked between the mountains and Resurrection Bay.

Writing Kate's story was a challenge. She's been one of my favorite of the Dawson siblings since I came up with the series idea (although probably they're all my favorite at different times), but when it came time to write her book, it was hard to get her to open up to me as a character—she's not an easy woman to figure out. It got me thinking about how different we all are, as I started thinking about the people Kate reminds me of, and my own personality differences from her. I love the way God made us all so unique and this book was a lot of fun because I got to make what I feel like is a pretty unique heroine. I wish Kate was real; I'd see if she'd go hiking with me and teach me some of her back-country skills.

One facet of Kate's personality was the way she was shaped by trauma in her past. We all have our own levels of grief and it takes just as much bravery to work through the ones in your life as it did for Kate to face that avalanche. I hope and pray that whatever you've faced in your past, you come to see how God can use it for good and that it brings you closer to Him.

I love hearing from readers! I can't tell you how many times I've had a challenging writing week and then opened my computer to find an encouraging letter from a reader. You can email me at sarahvarland@gmail.com, or you can find me online at facebook.com/sarahvarlandauthor, where I post writing news and a lot of Alaska photos.

Sara Varland

Get 4 FREE REWARDS!

We'll send you 2 FREE Books plus 2 FREE Mystery Gifts.

Love Inspired® books feature contemporary inspirational romances with Christian characters facing the challenges of life and love.

FREE Value Over **$20**

Get 4 FREE REWARDS!

We'll send you 2 FREE Books plus 2 FREE Mystery Gifts.

Harlequin® Heartwarming™ **Larger-Print** books feature traditional values of home, family, community and—most of all—love.

FREE Value Over **$20**
